Mountain Boy

The Adventures Of Orion Saddler

By
Norman D. Mullins

Woodland Press, LLC

Woodland Press, LLC
Chapmanville, WV

Dedication

To Hilary and Doug who have been a defining presence in my life.

Without encouragement from my wife, Hilary, this book would still be inside my head, forever dormant. I'm grateful for her tireless editing and encouragement which emboldened my efforts to share Orion with young people.

A special thanks goes to a unique group of students — Justin Baldwin, Brittany Cook, Alissa Dumm, Tyrell Love, Dylan Moore, and Beth Neely — all students at Cotton Belt Elementary School in York, South Carolina. These young people served as a book review panel, and approached their role with much enthusiasm. They provided many helpful comments and encouraged me to finish the book as soon as I could.

It was a sheer delight to watch their creative minds at work as they dug deeper and deeper into Orion's transition from a troubled boy to a young person with purpose.

FOREWORD

Orion Saddler yells, "Next time you see me, you won't know me too well!" to school officials as he heads home for the summer. His friends react wildly because Orion's bravado serves notice that he will be back in the fall more troublesome than ever. Although he doesn't know it, this verbal onslaught signals a crucial change in his life — the next time his buddies see him, he is a different person.

Concerned that their son is drifting toward serious trouble, Orion's parents send him to stay with his grandparents on a remote farm in West Virginia. Shortly after arriving, an assortment of adventures provides him with opportunities to expand his physical and emotional boundaries.

Orion's relationship with his grandparents, Poppy John and Mammaw Saddler, slowly deepens as they guide him through the ups and downs of farm life with love, discipline, and freedom. Poppy John's intimate knowledge of Saddler Mountain's secrets dazzles Orion, and his willingness to share that knowledge conveys a special trust in Orion — a trust that Orion develops into a growing respect for himself.

Mammaw's influence is both subtle and lasting. Her gentle and loving nature captures Orion's softer side enabling him to become more open, especially with adults.

In September, Orion returns home much tougher, but with a twist — he wants to take on the challenge of doing well in school. An unforgettable summer changed an immature, mischievous boy into a maturing young person who wants to become all he can be.

Published In Beautiful West Virginia
Woodland Press LLC
Appalachian Stories. Appalachian Authors. Appalachian Pride.
http://www.woodlandpress.com

SAN: 2 5 4 – 9 9 9

4

Mountain Boy
Table Of Contents

1
Going To The Farm

"Are we there yet?" Orion grumbled to his father only minutes into the four-hour-long trip from Ohio.

His father slowed the car down, looked over his right shoulder, and answered sharply, "Orion, that's the fourth time you've asked that question in the past forty-five minutes! Now find something to do to keep yourself busy! We have a long way to go."

His father was concentrating on driving and listening to the radio. He didn't seem to hear him as Orion mumbled, "Whoever would want to live all the way out in the boonies anyway?"

Orion and his father, Jesse Saddler, were on their way to the Saddler family farm in the highlands of West Virginia. Jesse had been born and raised there, but had spent the last twenty-five years in the Army.

Orion had tried to entertain himself in the car. Watching the passing countryside provided a diversion at first, but quickly got boring. Trees, bushes, railroad tracks, and houses soon melted into a continuous blur. Scenery passing by at fifty-five miles an hour, no matter how beautiful, didn't hold Orion's attention for very long. Too much talking or singing tended to get on his father's nerves, so he tried to be as quiet as possible.

He tried to count telephone poles, but started over several times because the poles went by too fast. Then Orion started counting the number of old barns that had "Chew Mail Pouch Tobacco" painted in huge letters across their sides, but gave up after losing track of the number for the third time.

A couple of brief rest stops relieved the monotony and gave him time to stretch his legs.

When he became tired of entertaining himself, napping took up some of his time. As he drifted off to sleep, he began thinking about his mother, who had stayed home alone. "No doubt, she wanted to avoid this incredibly long, boring trip," he thought.

Orion comforted himself as he nodded off by fondly remembering the many times she had told him, "I named you after the most beautiful stars in the heavens — the constellation Orion. God was happy on the day He made those stars because they are so beautiful, and He made you beautiful just to make me happy."

When they had passed the Ohio state line, crossing into West Virginia, his father repeatedly blew the horn. The honking startled Orion. He sat up straight in the seat and asked, "What did we hit?"

"Nothing. We just passed the West Virginia state line, and I'm home! Hallelujah!"

"Home? You live in Ohio, remember!"

Orion's cynical tone did not dampen his father's joyous feelings at being home again. Jesse simply explained, "Honking your horn whenever you cross the West Virginia state line signals that you're home at last."

Orion looked around and wondered if driving too long had gotten to his father and made him act strangely.

"Why would you be glad about coming home to this place? I don't see anything but mountains."

"It's hard to understand if you've not been raised here, but after you've been here a while you'll understand. Regardless of how long a West Virginian is gone or where or how far he's traveled, West Virginia is always home. Have you ever heard the expression, 'You can take a person out of the country, but you can't take the country out of the person?' Just substitute 'West Virginia' for 'country,' and it would describe me perfectly. I'm a West Virginian — always have been, always will be, and proud of it!"

The last comment convinced Orion that his father had indeed driven too long, and that it had taken its toll on his mental faculties. Hoping to change the subject, he stated indifferently, "You're right — it is hard to understand."

He decided not to ask any more questions, but sneered silently, "Always home? This place? It will never be home to me!"

Later as they began to get closer to their destination, Orion was amused that their car had passed the same stand of trees three times because of the way the steep, curvy road winded around the mountain. They had traveled nearly a mile uphill without seeming to get anywhere.

"The person who designed this road must have had a good sense of humor," he mused.

Because of his father's frequent moves with the Army, Orion had never been able to visit his grandparents. His parents had told him that visiting them this summer would help everyone get acquainted. However, this was not the real reason he was on the way to the farm.

In the past year, Orion's behavior had gotten worse, his grades had fallen dramatically, and he had started hanging out with the wrong crowd at school. His latest run-in with school officials was the last straw: being disrespectful to a teacher. When asked to move along to class by a teacher, Orion mumbled under his breath, "I'll move along if you get your big butt out of the way!"

Although the teacher did not hear exactly what Orion had said, she detected the disrespectful tone and took him to the office immediately. The principal sent him home for three days. As Orion left the office, the principal warned, "Young man, you're out of here for good if you get into trouble again!"

Orion's parents grounded him, restricting him to the house not only for the three days of suspension, but also for the next five weekends, as well. Other than going to school, he hadn't been out of the house for more than a month. Orion thought they were making a big deal out of nothing.

Jesse and Amanda Saddler had been concerned about their son's behavior and attitude for some time. They had not raised their son to be disrespectful to teachers or other authority figures, so this was the final straw. They decided to send him to the family farm — far away from his friends and other temptations. If anyone could help Orion, it would be Poppy John and Mammaw Saddler, his grandparents.

Orion's mother affectionately called Poppy John and Mammaw Saddler "mountain folk." They had lived their entire lives in the mountains of West Virginia. Neither one had ever traveled more than fifty miles from where they were born, nor would they ever. Their life was hard, but in a curious way, satisfying. Except for a few store-bought items, the farm provided most of their essential needs. It was something they were proud of.

They had raised a large family — five girls and seven boys — in the shelter of this deep mountain valley. The children were now spread throughout the country pursuing various careers and raising families of their own. There was one thing Poppy John and Mammaw knew how to do well: raise children the right way.

Orion did not want to be away from his buddies for the whole summer and thought the three-months' absence from Cleveland, friends, and familiar routines would be a complete waste of time. He had little enthusiasm for getting to know mountain folk, even if they were his grandparents.

Orion and his gang of friends called themselves "The Fifth Street Tigers." Although they were not violent, the members nonetheless had their moments of mischief at school and on the streets.

As Orion wondered to himself, he had no idea what it would be like spending so much time with two old people he didn't know, in some God-forsaken place nobody had ever heard of.

"Now, you call your grandparents 'Mammaw' and 'Poppy John' because that's what everyone calls them," his father had instructed him before they left.

Orion thought the names were funny, and he commented sarcastically, "If that's what they want to be called, it isn't any skin off my nose." His father chose to ignore the smart remark.

The Saddler farm was five miles from the main road, and there was no way to get a car up the steep mountainous path; so Jesse had to park the car at the bottom, and he and Orion had to walk the rest of the way. Orion secretly admired his father's strength as he watched him effortlessly carry the large box loaded with Orion's belongings, while he himself barely managed to lug the sack full of clothes over his back.

He was glad he had remembered to stuff his baseball glove and ball in the bag at the last minute, because he figured he would need them more than ever this summer, with nothing else to do.

The path they were walking on was narrow and twisting, stretching as far as Orion could see. "This reminds me of Little Red Riding Hood going through the woods to see her grandmother," he shouted to his father. He looked around and hoped there wasn't a big bad wolf hiding behind a tree.

"There are so many places a wolf could hide," Orion said halfseriously. "Trees are everywhere — something big and bad could be hiding behind any of them." His father didn't comment.

A few moments later, Orion heard his father's voice breaking through his daydreaming: "Hurry up, Orion! We've got to make it to the farm before dark."

"I'm hurrying just as fast as I can!"

It seemed to Orion that the surroundings changed with each step. As he looked around, different trees, shrubs, and flowers came into view. He reached down to touch a spring flower, but thought he'd better not pause that long. He needed to pay attention to what he was doing because he had been falling farther behind. He didn't want to be left alone, especially since there might be wolves and other ferocious animals roaming about.

His eyes wandered across to the next valley, where he saw a wall of pure green mixed with the colors of a thousand rainbows. He stopped momentarily to take it all in. The scene was so striking that he thought for a moment that his eyes were playing tricks on him.

"There's so much to see. I wonder what the names of all those trees and flowers might be," he reflected, as he inched along on the narrow path.

"I should have paid more attention in school!"

Orion was not a serious student. His teachers had told his parents that although he had a good mind, he didn't use it. He sometimes slept in class and, when awake, his mind wandered everywhere but to the lesson.

The sounds of the woods reminded him that he had left his dog, Patch, behind. "Patch would find the woods a huge playground," he thought. He wanted to bring him, but his father had told him that there were plenty of animals on the farm to play with.

This did not sit well with Orion. "Who wants to sit around talking to two old people and a bunch of dumb farm animals a zillion miles from nowhere?" he mumbled.

The farm had many animals — a horse, ten pigs, fifty chickens, twelve ducks, five cows, three "red-bone" hound dogs, a one-eyed goat, and one mean rooster named Rojo. Jesse had given his son the "lowdown" on each animal — which ones were friendly and which ones to avoid.

Orion was not anxious to meet any of the animals, but he did have a special interest in red-bone hound dogs because he had never seen one. "What's a red-bone hound dog?" Orion had asked.

"A red-bone hound dog is a special breed — born and bred to hunt, for generations. There's no other dog like a red-bone. A red-bone hound dog is the Cadillac of hunting dogs. They can find anything — beast or human — in these mountains."

"Humans? Why would dogs hunt humans?" Orion didn't like the sound of that.

"People get lost in these mountains if they're not careful," Jesse had said, emphasizing the word "careful."

Orion's dog was a mutt, so he was anxious to see what a dog that was specially bred looked like. Jesse had told him that his main job on the farm would be to take care of all the animals, with one exception: He was not to go near Rojo the rooster. His grandfather didn't let anyone mess with his rooster. That was all right with Orion. Who would want to baby-sit a mean chicken with a bad attitude?

He also couldn't imagine a one-eyed goat being much fun either but, according to his father, the goat had special talents that would come in handy this summer; and, Jesse promised, Orion would be thankful for having made friends with him.

Jesse also warned him about poisonous copperheads and rattlesnakes slithering in the underbrush, so he would always have to be alert and very careful. Orion didn't know much about snakes, but he knew enough not to step on them or get too close to them.

Orion threw the bag of clothes over his right shoulder and moved a little faster. It seemed that his mother had packed enough clothes, mostly jeans and T-shirts, to last him for several years. The clothes were heavy but Orion didn't complain, because he knew it wouldn't have done any good. After shifting the load, he shouted to his father, "Wait for me!"

Barely in sight, his father stopped and shouted, "Catch up, Orion! You're falling too far behind. We've still got an hour to go."

"An hour! Darn!"

"What?"

"Nothing! I was thinking that an hour is a long time."

"Not as long as it has been!" Jesse said with a half-smile, "We have to hurry if we want to avoid the She-Devil Black Panther."

Orion stopped dead in his tracks and nervously exclaimed, "She-Devil Black Panther? What panther? You didn't tell me about a black panther!" Suddenly, he found that he had lots of energy, and he scampered as fast as he could to catch up with his father. The mentioning of a black panther — a She-Devil at that — was more than enough motivation to move faster. He couldn't think of anything worse than a devil.

"There's always been talk in these mountains of a mysterious black creature that roams at night looking for prey, so everyone gets home before dark. And that includes us," Jesse said in a very serious tone.

Orion remembered vaguely studying about mountain lions in

school, but not panthers. Wasn't that the big cat that lived somewhere in South America, that killed crocodiles for fun? But this was not South America. This was West Virginia.

"What in the world is a She-Devil Panther?" Orion asked his father.

"It's like a mountain lion, only bigger and stronger. It's also black from head to toe. The legend has it that someone brought this panther from South America as a pet, but she escaped shortly after arriving. Ever since, the panther has been roaming these hills at night scaring everyone to death."

"But South America is beyond Florida, isn't it?" Orion nervously tried to ask. He couldn't imagine anything beyond Florida, because Florida was practically the end of the world to him.

"Yes. It's far, far away — even from Florida."

A few minutes passed as Orion rolled over in his mind the possibility of a black panther being so far from home, then he asked hopefully, "You're kidding about that She-Devil Black Panther, right?"

"Well, I'm not sure if I'm kidding or not. I've never seen her. But when traveling in these mountains, I always take the stories of the black panther seriously. Your Poppy John swears that she roams these hills looking for unsuspecting travelers, especially young boys."

"Young boys! What does she want with young boys?" Orion barely managed to ask.

"The panther takes little boys so she can raise them, because she doesn't have any young ones of her own. When she's out roaming, you can hear her sad wail all over these mountains. She's everywhere. Dogs can't pick up her scent most of the time, but when they do, they refuse to follow it because she's so vicious."

"Having a pedigree doesn't do those red-bone hound dogs any good if they can't track a She-Devil Black Panther!" Orion remarked.

Jesse smiled, then went on: "Lots of folks have seen her silhouette in the moonlight with a young boy running beside her. They say that She-Devil is so black you can only see her blazing yellow eyes. On a moonless night, she could be right beside you, and you would never see her."

Jesse saw the anxiety rising in his son's eyes, then quickly added, "But you don't have to worry; you're a tad too old and set in your ways for a She-Devil to raise. Besides, your mamma wouldn't take too kindly to that."

"How old is too old? If she catches an older boy, what does she do with him?" Orion asked, his voice trembling.

"Oh, I guess you're too old if you are around ten or eleven. And besides, we don't have to worry about that black panther until dark. She only comes out at night. But I pity anyone who's caught out alone around here after dark. Many people have started somewhere after the sun went down, and they've never been heard from or seen again."

Orion was not surprised that people perished in these woods at night. Even in the daylight, the woods were dark and eerie. As he looked around, his mind wandered: Tree limbs suddenly became giant arms reaching out to grab him; flowers turned into poisonous pools devouring the flesh of small boys. The winding path ahead became a gigantic snake, grabbing weary travelers around the ankles, then slowly making its way up their bodies until…!

"Orion, pay attention! You almost slipped off the side of the mountain!"

"Yes, sir," Orion responded, regaining his balance.

He certainly had no intention of falling a thousand feet to the small stream below or, for that matter, being in the mountains after the sun went down. So he crossed his eyes and legs, spit on his fingers, hit his hands together three times, and swore he would never be alone in the woods after dark.

By now, Orion wanted to forget about that boy-stealing black panther, but he had to know more. He waited about ten minutes, as his mind replayed everything he'd just heard, and then blurted out,

"Why did that She-Devil stay in West Virginia anyway? I'm sure she would have gotten lonely without other panthers around!"

"I don't know. But if this panther is as mean as everybody says, she can do just about anything she pleases," his father said.

Then Jesse casually mentioned something else that caught Orion's attention, "Even with the She-Devil Black Panther prowling at night, the mountain trail is still a much better way to travel than sloshing through the Pawpaw to get to the farm."

Orion didn't like the way his father said "the Pawpaw," and he felt a big lump rise in his throat as he muttered, "What's the Pawpaw?" After the black panther scare, he really didn't want to hear what his father was going to tell him, but it was too late.

His father explained, "A pawpaw is a tree with a small fruit that turns black when it ripens. Mountain folks like to eat them; they taste a little like a banana. 'The Pawpaw' is a place several miles from the farm. It's like a jungle with water, pawpaw trees, plants of every kind, and plenty of snakes — especially copperheads. The thickness of the greenery blocks the sunshine, so it's almost always dark. It takes you a half day to get through the Pawpaw, at least in one piece."

Jesse continued, "But the mystery of the Pawpaw isn't in the tree or the fruit. Hardly anyone travels through the Pawpaw anymore because of all the eerie sounds. The place is full of who knows what. If you listen carefully, especially on windy or rainy days, you can hear sounds that will make you shiver and shake in your boots."

The comment about eerie sounds put the conversation on another level. Mentioning a roaming She-Devil Panther was one thing, but creepy sounds in a dark, wet place was something all together different. Orion gasped as he tried to speak. Not a word came out of his mouth even though he thought he was speaking distinctly. His hands shook so much that the bag of clothes almost slipped to the ground. As he tightened his grip, he stumbled but, thankfully, didn't fall.

He hoped his father didn't see the clumsiness, as he asked,

"What makes the strange sounds?"

"I believe it's just from all the tree branches hitting against one another, and the birds and other animals wandering in and out. Regardless, though, it's not a place you want to find yourself all alone. I'm sure Poppy John will have something to say about that, too."

Orion thought sarcastically, "Of course he will. Grown-ups always tell you what to do. They don't think a kid like me has any brains. They think they know everything!"

After his father's description, Orion thought the Pawpaw would be a great place to explore. He asked, "Have you ever been through the Pawpaw yourself, Dad?"

"Many times, when I was too young and too fearless for my own good. Now, no more questions. We have to pay attention to what we're doing. Ask Poppy John about the She-Devil Black Panther and the Pawpaw when we get there. He knows everything there is to know about them."

Orion fell silent. Then he added, "There seems to be a lot of weird things happening in these mountains!"

"Not any more than in Cleveland," his father responded.

"Yeah, but it's still a scary thought." Orion then and there decided to stay close to his father, or at least to keep him in sight. As long as he could see his father, he would be all right. He started paying attention to every sound, not really sure of what he was listening for.

A chirping bird immediately caught Orion's attention. He wondered if birds, always on the wing, ever saw the She-Devil Black Panther preying on young boys. They were certainly high enough in the sky to see everything, but he doubted if birds would be much help. They were always busy hunting for food.

He tried to chirp back to the bird, but with little success. That, however, didn't keep him from trying.

The path was getting steep. The more Orion tried to keep up, the more he fell behind. And the more he fell behind, the more difficult it became to take another step. He shouted to his father in desperation, "I need a rest! My feet are killing me!"

"OK, I guess we can spare a few minutes. It has been a rough trip."

Orion sighed and said, "Thank you," then threw himself on the ground. He pulled a Fifth Avenue candy bar out of his pocket, took a big bite and laid his head gently on the clothes bag.

"Now don't go to sleep. We've got one more rough section ahead, then we'll be able to see the farm," his father promised.

Orion had a special talent: being able to go to sleep anywhere at the drop of a hat. Everyone marveled at this ability, but he didn't think much of it. He didn't think that falling to sleep was a talent. Talent was something that came naturally, but required hard work to develop — like throwing a baseball as fast as Bob Feller.

"Now that Bob Feller has talent," he said out loud.

His dad's response surprised Orion: "I agree! Anyone who can throw a baseball a hundred miles an hour has as much talent as one human being can have."

Baseball was the one interest that Jesse and Orion had in common. They attended as many Cleveland Indians games as possible. But it would be different this summer. His beloved Indians would have to win the pennant without him.

Fifteen minutes later, Orion's father asked, "Ready to go?"

"Sure," Orion said, rubbing sleep from his eyes. This time he was ready to go all the way.

The time passed quickly as Orion took in all the sights. He had never seen so many beautiful flowers. They were everywhere, in every color — red, pink, purple, yellow, white, and other colors that he had never seen before. He decided he liked violets best because they looked so delicate and had such distinct coloring.

The violets brought to mind the ditty, "Roses are red, and violets are blue." He laughed and thought, "These violets are definitely not blue. The songwriter must have been more interested in rhyme than accuracy!"

Sure enough, when they topped the mountain, he could see the farmhouse in the distance. It was much bigger than he imagined, and he immediately spotted the large stream that ran in front of the house.

"I'll have a great time swimming this summer," he thought. The thought of swimming in the afternoon pleased Orion very much: "What a way to spend a lazy afternoon, soaking up sunshine and drinking a cold RC Cola." Orion didn't know it at the time, but R C Colas were not on the summer menu. As a matter of fact, he would not get the chance to enjoy his favorite cold soft drink again — or any other one, for that matter — until fall.

As they walked on, Orion kept his eyes glued on the farm. He saw the barn and what he assumed were the chicken coop and pig-pen. He saw Prince, Poppy John's plow horse, standing beside the stream. Prince was gigantic, even from a distance. "Wow! How can a horse be so big?"

His father answered, "Prince has worked hard all his life, so every ounce is muscle."

His father went on, "There are two things to remember about Prince: first, he is not overly friendly; and second, he's hard-headed about doing anything except what he's used to doing — pulling a plow."

Orion replied with a laugh, "I guess he feels like plowing is enough."

"Maybe. Although Prince won't hurt you, he can make your life miserable if you let him."

Orion couldn't believe that a dumb old horse even had a mind, let alone be smart enough to try to make him miserable. He shrugged his shoulders and said, "I don't plan to let a plow horse upset me!"

Jesse snickered as he said, "I bet Prince will be glad to hear that!"

The closer Orion got to the farm, the more questions about this upcoming summer adventure kept racing through his head: "Who are these old people anyway? I don't have to like them just because they're my grandparents, do I? What in the world am I going to do to keep myself busy all summer long?"

As the farmhouse came into sight, Orion saw smoke rising from its chimney; then he heard a bell. He excitedly asked his father, "Why is that bell ringing?"

His father smiled and said, "When you hear that bell, it means supper's almost ready. Your Mammaw has been at the stove all afternoon. You'll have the meal of your life tonight."

"I can't wait. I could eat a horse right now!"

"Well, don't say that in front of old Prince. He already thinks the whole world's against him," Orion's father said with a laugh.

"Yes, sir."

"Remember that every time you hear the bell, you head back to the house no matter where you are or what you're doing. Poppy John doesn't like to be kept waiting for his meals."

"Yes, sir. I'll remember," Orion answered, but he was thinking, "Why is that not a surprise? And I'll bet he will want me to wait on him hand and foot, too! Just you wait and see! I've got a surprise for him: I don't wait on anybody!"

About thirty yards from the house, Orion saw a huge man come through the front door. "That's your Poppy John. He looks as feisty as ever," Jesse told his son, with a smile.

Orion stopped dead in his tracks, as he stared at the huge man coming toward them at a fast pace.

Jesse turned to Orion and said, "Don't let that old man scare you. He's nothing but a big teddy bear."

Orion didn't know what to make of that comment. Poppy John sure didn't look like a teddy bear, but Orion still replied, "Yes, sir."

Orion didn't take his eyes off the big man as he approached. The closer they got to the house, the larger the man seemed to become. Orion had never seen a man that huge. Poppy John was a foot taller than his father and had hair as white as snow. "A teddy bear!" Orion whispered, "He looks more like a grizzly bear!"

When Orion and his father were about ten feet away, the big man smiled, threw up his hand and bellowed, "Welcome to God's Country!" He walked over and gave his grown son a big hug, almost lifting him off the ground. He then turned and, gazing at Orion, asked, "This your boy?"

"Yes, sir." This was the first time Orion had ever heard his father call anyone "sir."

"He's kind of puny, but Mammaw will take care of that." He grabbed Orion and gave him a hug so tight that Orion almost lost his breath.

"Yeah, his Mammaw will fix him up fine. You won't know him by the end of the summer."

Orion didn't like the word "puny," but he didn't dare say anything to a man who was four times bigger than he was.

"You're late. I thought I'd have to send the dogs after you," Poppy John quizzed them, as he took Orion's bag.

"We got a late start from home," Jesse replied. "Then the car overheated on Megan Mountain, and we had to let her rest a spell."

"Darn cars! Give me a good old horse any day," Poppy John said excitedly. Before Jesse could say anything, Poppy John threw his arms in the air and exclaimed, "Don't start telling me how much things are changing. I've still got two good eyes, and I'm doing OK with a plow horse and two good feet. Isn't that right, Boy?"

Before Orion realized that his grandfather was talking to him, Jesse and Poppy John were walking arm in arm toward the house. He heard his grandfather ask his father something in a hushed voice. Jesse answered him, "No, but I heard some strange sounds close to the live oak tree at Wilson's Branch."

"That Devil is ten times meaner than Ole Lucifer and twice as smart. She always liked that live oak tree," his grandfather said loudly. "I figure she's raised two or three boys there. I'm going to whack that tree down someday just to annoy that mountain Devil!"

Poppy John made an abrupt turn and called out to Orion, "Come on, Boy, Mammaw's got supper on the table! We don't want to be late."

"Yes, sir," Orion answered meekly. He wasn't ready to call a perfect stranger "Poppy John."

Although Orion was hungry, food was not on his mind. His head was spinning from tales of the She-Devil Black Panther; mysterious sounds in the Pawpaw; creepy crawling snakes; farm animals with odd personalities; and this huge man, who insisted on being called "Poppy John."

"How did I get myself into this mess, and how in the world will I ever get use to these strange people?" he wondered.

Orion looked around and saw all the farm animals — the cows, the goat, the horse, the ducks, and the pigs — lined up, watching his every move. He amused himself as he wondered if this was the official greeting committee; he smiled, waved, and said, "Thank you, thank you, all you farm animals. But where is the welcoming band? Shouldn't I at least be greeted with trumpets?" The animals didn't even move in response.

"I wonder if they've ever seen a stranger?" Orion thought, and then answered his own question, "Probably not. No one else could ever find this place."

Orion took one more look around, sighed, and thought reluctantly, "Since this will be my home for the next few months, I might as well make the best of it."

Orion didn't exactly love living in Cleveland that much, but it sure sounded good at the moment. Being stuck on a remote West Virginia farm with no one around for miles was going to be nothing like living in a crowded city in Ohio.

He couldn't explain why, but the more he thought about it, the more he couldn't wait to see what tomorrow would bring.

2

Fighting A Champion Rooster

After saying goodbye to his father the next morning, Orion looked around at what would be his home for the next three months. The trees looked like giant stick men through Orion's sleepy eyes, and his ears were especially sensitive to the busy chatter of the farm animals. He noted that this was the first time he had ever actually witnessed the dawn of a new day.

Orion wondered if he should wait for his grandfather to tell him what to do or just go back to bed. Still sleepy, he muttered, "I might as well go back to bed," but Poppy John showed up as soon as the words came out of his mouth.

Poppy John put his arm around Orion's shoulder and commented as they headed toward the barn, "Boy, as long as you're awake, we might as well go to work. On the farm, we work as long as there's work to be done, and that's usually from sunup to sundown, six days a week. But after you finish the chores you can explore Saddler Mountain or do whatever you want. Just let Mammaw or me know where you're going."

Poppy John continued, "Oh, by the way, bedtime for us is eight o'clock, but you can go to bed whenever you get sleepy. That is, after you've finished the chores."

"What a relief!" Orion thought. He hadn't been in bed at eight since first grade. He then asked, "Are you sure there will be time to explore after I finish the chores?"

Poppy John grinned and said, "We'll see how it goes. One last thing to remember: Don't pay attention to the no-work bird."

"The what-kind-of-bird?"

"The no-work bird!"

"What's that?"

"A very odd bird that has declared that every day is 'National No

23

Work Day,' and doesn't want anyone to work at any time for any reason. He sits in a tree near where you're working and sings 'no work' continuously. It'll drive you crazy, but there are only two ways to make him stop: stop working, or throw a rock at him."

"I'd stop working," Orion responded in a cocky manner, as if he had a chip on his shoulder.

Poppy John smiled and said, "I tried that once, but the bird sat there waiting for me to start working again. If I moved, he moved. If I started working, he started singing. If I hid, he was waiting when I reappeared. There was no getting away from him. However, I found that a rock whizzing past his head put him on the run, at least for a while.

"Anyway, you'll have to figure out the best strategy for you. You might even like his silly song. But now it's time to show you the farm and introduce you to the animals."

After the tour of the farm and a demonstration of daily chores, Poppy John patted Orion on the back and said, "OK, Boy, you're on your own. Remember: Watch out for that no good no-work bird."

Orion suddenly felt isolated as he watched his grandfather walk away laughing, but nonetheless commented to himself, "The no-work bird, ha! Like there really is such a bird. He must think I'm really dumb to fall for that one."

He saw Poppy John's plow horse out of the corner of his eye moving his mouth in an exaggerated way, as he made funny sounds. "Look at that dumb horse — he's making fun of me!" Orion said to himself. He shrugged his shoulders and mumbled, "I guess this is the way it's going to be here since I'm the new kid on the block. But that's OK. I can take it."

It took Orion a week to get the work routine down pat. His main task was to feed the animals and to make sure they had enough water throughout the day. Cleaning the barn and pigpen on alternate days rounded out his list of chores.

Orion's first attempts at communication with his grandparents were awkward until he stopped using his usual city jargon. One day

Poppy John asked, "How do you like Rojo?"

"Oh, he's a real cool cat!" Orion answered.

"A real cool cat? But he's not a cat, and I don't think he's staying very cool on hot days like this," commented his grandfather.

"I didn't mean he's a real cat."

"Then why did you call him a cat?"

"It's just an expression that we use."

"But he doesn't look like a cat."

Frustrated, Orion tried one more time to get his grandfather to understand, "Of course a rooster doesn't look like a cat. And I'm sure he's not cool, as far as the temperature goes, at the present time. But his fighting ability and proud strut make him different from other animals in the barnyard."

"Well, he's certainly different — but being different from an ordinary rooster makes him a cool cat?"

"Yes, that's it! He's different all right," Orion added, "and he knows it, too."

Poppy John's eyes lit up as he said, "Oh, I think I get it. He's not a cat, and he's not cool, but he's a cool cat."

Orion said under his breath, "It's about time."

Orion got rid of the hip language after the cool cat incident, and instead stuck to ordinary, everyday language.

One morning several weeks after his arrival, Orion felt a sharp tap on the bottom of his left foot as he slept. Although it was not hard enough to send him scurrying for his pants, the sting woke him. His first thought was that it was too early to "rise and shine," as his grandmother urged each morning. He rolled over, half-heartedly mumbling to himself, "Must've been a dream."

The second tap felt more like a switch as it hit the tender part of his right foot. He started to yell, but heard his grandfather's voice at the foot of his bed, "Get up, Boy! You're not dreaming! I need you to get that rowdy rooster back in the coop before breakfast!"

"Yes, sir," Orion responded quickly. Although he was half asleep, he knew he had big problems .

"How in the world will I ever get that beast back in the coop?" Orion asked himself. Nothing came to mind.

This was the first time Poppy John had asked Orion to take care of his champion rooster. He considered it a tribute that his grandfather had given him this responsibility; however, chasing a bad-tempered rooster was not his idea of how to start the day.

Before you could say "the cat scat with a flat hat" three times, Orion was on his feet, looking for his pants. Somehow he managed to say in a deep voice, "The champ jumped camp, uh? Don't worry, I'll get that chicken back in the coop in a hurry!"

"The champ jumped camp! I like that! I'll have to tell Mammaw that one," Poppy John commented, as he slapped his knee and laughed uncontrollably.

"Might want to wear long sleeves and pants, Boy. That old bird's likely as not to be hungry, and you might look like a good meal this morning."

Orion rubbed his eyes and saw his grandfather's huge red bandana swinging from the back pocket of his bib overalls as he left the room laughing and repeating, "The champ jumped camp! That Boy sure has a way with words. Mammaw, I've got a good one for you this morning!"

Orion didn't find being a meal for the meanest rooster in Grace County all that funny. As he stumbled over his shoes, he could still hear his grandfather laughing down the hallway.

Most people think roosters are cute creatures that provide wake-up service at the crack of dawn with a loud cock-a-doodle-do. But not this rooster! Beautiful sunrises came and went undetected because he refused to cock-a-doodle-do like a normal rooster. All this one wanted to do was fight and, of course, strut around the yard like he was Master of the Universe.

Poppy John named the rooster "Rojo," which means "red" in Spanish. The crown on the top of his head was as red as the sunset, and his feathers were also different shades of red. Rojo's tail feathers, however, were his crowning glory. They rose magnificently from his rear end and spread out when he strutted. He was a sight to behold, but it wasn't a sight Orion wanted to see at the moment.

When Rojo wasn't strutting, he stayed in the back corner of the chicken pen, yapping, pecking the ground, and fluffing his wings. He never let anyone near him, not even other chickens. It was not a smart idea to approach him, and touching him was out of the question. Even Poppy John had to throw a net over his head when he took him to a cockfight, so you could say he didn't have a friendly bone in his whole body.

Poppy John purchased Rojo from a stranger who brought him all the way from Mexico. This poor fellow happened to wander through the mountains after his jalopy had completely quit on him, when he then set out on foot with his few possessions — nearly flat broke, hungry, and exhausted. Poppy John, always ready to help a person in trouble, bought the rooster for a few dollars and four ham biscuits.

Poppy John called Rojo "the most beautiful of all God's creatures." Orion called him "dumb," because how could you not be a little dense when your whole purpose in life was to fight to the death?

Rojo's long beak didn't concern Orion; however, the rooster's claws did pose a serious problem. They were two inches long, sharp as a razor, and Rojo used them as a deadly weapon. Orion once observed, "I don't see how that chicken walks with claws like that — he could climb a tree with ease."

Many tales had circulated about the fabulous Mexican bird. Orion liked the baseball story best. It seems that a teenager threw a baseball at Rojo during a cockfight. The rooster caught the ball like Joe DiMaggio snaring a high fly ball in center field. He then threw the baseball back, without missing a beat, hitting the kid in the head.

However, Rojo's ability to throw that baseball didn't keep Orion from throwing rocks at him and calling him unpleasant names every chance he got. When Rojo looked the other way, Orion would send him running by whizzing a rock at him and shouting, "Let's see if you can catch this, birdbrain!" Needless to say it was not a nice thing to do and, later, Orion would find that the "chickens would come home to roost," so to speak.

One day, Orion mentioned Rojo to his grandmother: "I don't know where Mexico is, but it must be far away. Maybe that's why that rooster is so unfriendly. I would be too if I was that far from home and couldn't understand a word people were saying. But that's really no excuse for being downright ornery."

His grandmother smiled and said, "Be patient, everything works out for the best. And perhaps if you didn't throw rocks at him, he might be a little more friendly." His cheeks red with embarrassment, Orion realized that he had just been rebuked for something he should not have been doing, but he didn't say a word. He wondered how his grandmother knew about the rock throwing.

Orion finished dressing, making sure his overalls and brogans were tightly secured. He didn't want that rooster to slice his legs and feet with his claws. Satisfied that he was well protected, he looked around the room for a weapon, something to fend off that monster. He didn't see anything. Then he remembered a big walking stick on the front porch.

He ran out to the front porch. His stomach growling and hurrying him along, Orion didn't want a grumpy rooster to interfere with his enjoying Mammaw's special breakfast.

As he picked up the walking stick, a noise came from the direction of the live oak tree near the barn. He whirled around. Sure enough, there was the rooster pecking at the ground and yapping away. "My luck's still holding," Orion said in a whisper. "He's looking the other way."

Orion stepped off the porch, assuming a warrior crouch. "I should have put on some war paint," he said, with a self-assured grin. Still staring straight at Rojo, he put the stick in his left hand and picked up a rock. His movement was quiet and sure. Orion was the model of strength and courage. He knew what he had to do. As he got closer, his steps got slower and more deliberate.

When he got about twenty feet away from his opponent, he looked back to make sure the house was still close behind him. When he turned back in the direction of the rooster, his heart nearly stopped as he shrieked, "OH, MY GOSH!"

Rojo had turned around, facing him. Orion tightened his grip on the walking stick, confidently shouting, "Let's see you get up on this," as he swung it through the air in a mighty threatening gesture.

He continued with his bravado, "You're just like every other big shot I know! Always threatening people and putting them down! Always thinking you're better than everybody else! Well, here's one person who's about to show Mr. Big Shot a thing or two!"

He raised the rock to throw just as Rojo began scratching the ground with his enormous claws, like a bull getting ready to charge. Poppy John had told him about bullfighting — how the bull would dig his feet in the ground and snort loudly before charging the bullfighter. Poppy John said the bullfighter must stand his ground as the crazy 2000-pound beast heads directly at him. At the very last second, the bullfighter then moves to the side with his red cape flowing triumphantly in the wind.

The people in the stadium would cheer crazily at the bullfighter's courage each time the bull passed him. After a short time, the brightly clad bullfighter would finish him off with a swift blow from his trusty sword.

"How difficult could that be?" Orion boldly wondered.

Orion thought the bullfighting strategy was a good one to use on his barnyard foe. He would stand and face his archenemy without moving a muscle. The stick would be his sword, and his cunning and intelligence would be the difference between him and this dumb chicken. He was sure that this approach would unnerve Rojo. He would whack Rojo at just the right time, and that would be that.

From then on, it would just be a matter of intimidating Rojo into going back inside the chicken coop. Orion thought it would be a piece of cake to send that chicken scurrying back where he belonged.

Orion looked directly into the creature's eyes. Besides being as big as saucers, Rojo's eyes were fierce and as red as his feathers. Orion got a funny feeling in his stomach, like he was going to throw up. Knowing he had no choice but to move on, Orion started the attack by throwing the rock. It whizzed past Rojo's head.

"Missed! Darn!" The bird didn't move an inch in any direction, but kept on scratching the ground faster and faster.

Orion made more threatening gestures with his sword-stick as he looked directly in the eyes of the red monster.

Letting out a loud, eerie wail, Rojo started toward Orion, first, in a slow trot, and then gaining speed. His devilish eyes never left Orion's. Without breaking stride, Rojo then started screaming wildly. In hindsight, Orion realized the bird was squawking his version of "COCK-A-DOODLE-DO," but it was the strangest "COCK-A-DOODLE-DO" he had ever heard. Maybe it was in Spanish.

Orion stood his ground, not moving a muscle.

Orion knew the moment of truth was upon him. Actually, the moment of truth was now only a few feet away, bearing down hard, and coming right toward him.

It was then that Orion did what any red-blooded American boy would do in the same circumstances: He ran for his life! Thank goodness the front porch was only a short distance away.

Orion made it to the front porch, but not before he felt something grab the back of his leg. He screamed, "Oh, no!" and swung the stick around. He hit something, but he didn't look back as he jerked his leg free.

He giggled nervously when he ran through the front door, knowing that Rojo hadn't done any serious damage.

Before Orion could catch his breath, Poppy John shouted, "Got that rooster yet, Boy?"

Orion cleared his throat and answered, "No, sir. Not yet."

"Well, hurry. Time's wasting."

Orion sat down on the bed to catch his breath. He couldn't tell his grandfather that he had just run for his life from a chicken. The chicken happened to be a champion rooster, but he was still a chicken.

He looked down and saw the back leg of his trousers. They were in shreds. He let out with a big, "WHEEEW! That was close," and he laughed out loud again.

He wiped the sweat from his forehead and started thinking. Getting the rooster back in the pen had become a solemn matter — his honor was at stake, or, rather, his pride. He had to get the best of this dumb rooster. But how?

"What am I going to do? The bullfighting stuff didn't work," he thought, as doubts invaded his head. He would have to tell his grandfather he was afraid of the rooster if he didn't come up with something that would work. And he wanted to avoid his grandfather's disappointment at all costs. But as time quickly passed and the rumbles in his stomach became louder, the more desperate he became.

Deep in thought, Orion barely heard his grandfather call out again, "Boy, breakfast will be ready in a few minutes."

"OK, Poppy John, I'll be ready!"

At the moment, it seemed that getting Rojo back in the coop was as unlikely as seeing Prince jump over the moon.

He looked out the window and saw the rooster still near the front porch, pecking hard at the ground. Looking up every few seconds, Rojo would spread his wings, make an awful, threatening noise, and strut around in a circle.

"That must be his victory dance," Orion thought. He became more determined than ever not to let that show-off rooster have another victory dance at his expense.

As he watched Rojo, an idea popped into his head. Orion couldn't believe it — he had come up with a strategy that just might work.

"That's it!" he declared, as he slapped his hands together.

The answer to his problem came out of the blue. Feeling confident again, with a sudden burst of energy, Orion shook his fist at Rojo and said, "OK, birdbrain, let's see how ferocious you are now!"

But he had no time to waste. He quickly went into the back room to retrieve three objects: a hat and two sticks. The hat was big and bright with a floppy wide brim. Poppy John had also bought it from the man who brought Rojo from Mexico. He called it a sombrero. Orion thought it was the funniest hat he had ever seen. He had put it on once, but had felt self-conscious. It was so huge that it came down over his eyes. But now it would come in handy.

The two sticks were strong, straight, and sturdy, each almost three feet long. They were perfect for swords. Poppy John called them "baby sticks" because he had used them to measure the length of his sons and daughters when they had been born. Poppy John didn't have regular yardsticks, so he went out and found a strong sapling, cut it down, and marked it off to use for measuring his children as they grew. Each time, he would also mark the spot representing the child's height, along with the child's name & age. The baby sticks became keepsakes over the years.

On the way out of the room, Orion also grabbed a red scarf that belonged to his grandmother. A warrior about to engage the enemy always had something colorful to wear. He wasn't sure why. Maybe it was to get a lady's attention.

As he draped the scarf around his neck and left shoulder, Orion stopped at the front door to get his bearings. Rojo was there, still yapping and pecking the ground. Orion snickered; he couldn't help it.

"Just like a dumb chicken, running around like he had no brains whatsoever," he said loudly enough for the rooster to hear.

As he walked through the front door, Rojo's evil eyes were already on him. Orion smiled, looked the bird straight in his eyes, and said, "This is your last chance to surrender and return to the coop peacefully."

He pointed to the coop and said firmly, "Get back in that chicken coop while you still have some self-respect."

Rojo started scratching the ground much harder this time. His eyes were as cold as stone.

"Go ahead and start those silly noises. I'm not going anywhere," Orion said, leaning on one of the sticks.

Sure enough, Rojo started the strange cock-a-doodle-dooing.

"We'll have to give you voice lessons if you insist on yapping like some strange bird with the heebie jeebies!" Orion taunted.

He placed the sombrero in his right hand, grasped the two baby sticks, and jumped off the porch into the arena. Orion knew he looked good. With his red scarf blowing in the wind, he was ready for battle.

He moved quickly on his tiptoes several steps to the left. The tiptoe maneuver was just for show. Rojo matched him step for step. He took twenty more steps with his back to Rojo that placed him close to the chicken pen. The pageantry and boldness of Orion's moves puzzled Rojo, but he didn't make any threatening moves. Instead, he again imitated Orion's steps.

Orion opened the door to the chicken coop slowly, turned to face Rojo, and threw the sombrero down on the ground in front of the rooster. Rojo tilted his head, as he curiously approached the sombrero.

"That's right, chicken legs, now we dance!"

Orion began beating the sticks together and singing loudly, "La Cucaracha, la Cucaracha, ya no puedes caminar..."

Orion had no idea what the words meant, but he had heard Poppy John sing them so often that he knew the tune and the words by heart.

Rojo started strutting around the hat, seeming to keep time with the beat of Orion's song. Poppy John had told him that everybody in Mexico danced around a sombrero if "La Cucaracha" was played or sung. Orion reasoned that if every person did it, then a Mexican rooster might do it, too.

And he was right! The louder Orion bellowed out and beat on

those sticks, the faster Rojo circled the hat. Orion was having a great time watching him go in circles. Rojo seemed to be in a trance, having forgotten that Orion was close by.

"La Cucaracha, La Cucaracha..." the words kept coming. "La Cucaracha, La Cucaracha..." And the rooster kept strutting. On the eighth beat, Orion would click his heels, and shout "CARAMBA."

Although Orion was enjoying how silly the champion chicken looked going round in circles, his arms were tiring. He moved several steps to the left, putting himself between the sombrero and the chicken coop gate. The dance continued, louder and more colorful than ever.

Orion could feel the sweat popping out on his forehead. It was the moment of truth — would he show Rojo who was boss, or would he run again?

As Rojo went by him, Orion put both sticks in his right hand, lifted his voice dramatically, "LA CUCARACHA, LA CUCARACHA..."

As Rojo passed him a second time, Orion drew back the sticks, hit that rooster just as hard as he could right in the behind, and yelled, "Let's see you CUCARACHA now, chicken brain!"

The bird took flight right through the chicken coop gate, screaming a blood-curdling yell and landing on the far side of the lot. Orion rushed over and closed the gate. He threw his arms in the air and yelled, "Yeah! How do you like them apples?" Rojo didn't utter a sound. He dropped his head; he knew he had been thoroughly defeated.

Orion ran back to the house. As he entered the front door, Poppy John called out from the kitchen, "What was all that commotion, Boy?"

Orion smiled, and yelled back, "Nothing, Poppy John. Is breakfast ready?"

Orion straightened his shoulders, threw out his chest, and went in to wash up for breakfast with his grandparents. He was dying to share every detail of his victory, but he didn't think they would be interested in the finer points of outsmarting a rooster or that it would be proper to brag on himself. Now was not the time to strut his stuff. It was enough that Rojo was back in the chicken coop and that his job was well done.

However, Orion's skirmish with the meanest rooster in the county hadn't gotten by unnoticed. After dinner Orion overheard Poppy John commenting to Mammaw: "That Orion is already showing a great deal more responsibility! Getting that rooster back in the chicken coop took a lot of brains, as well as guts. He's a lot like his dad — he's got a good head on his shoulders."

As he secretly listened in on their conversation, Orion smiled at the thought of Poppy John watching the whole battle with Rojo.

"I bet he enjoyed every minute of it!" Orion almost said out loud, as he imagined Poppy John beaming with pride.

Mammaw agreed with Poppy John: "It'll take some time, but he's going to be all right. He's a good boy."

Little did Orion know it at the time, but the story of his conquering the fierce red monster that day would become Saddler family legend for generations to come.

3

Exploring The Pawpaw

Orion's victory over Rojo elevated his confidence to a ridiculous level. He was sure there was nothing he couldn't do, so the next morning after chores were done, he took off for the Pawpaw — alone. He didn't know what to expect, but the urge to find out why grown men avoided the site was too strong to wait until Poppy John found time to take him.

Besides, Orion was a little upset with Poppy John over the whole issue. He didn't like it too well when Poppy John had put down the law when he first arrived at the farm: "Boy, don't ever go into that place alone!"

Orion had taken that prohibition personally because he felt that Poppy John didn't think he could take care of himself. "He's just an old man who thinks I'm a little baby," he said. "What could be so dangerous about walking on a mountain path that's overgrown with trees, ferns, and other stuff? I'll show him!"

Poppy John had carefully explained how to walk on the slippery rocks in the Pawpaw: "The secret of not falling is to walk slowly, and when possible, stay next to the hill."

"Aha," Orion had thought, " If he didn't want me to go, why did he explain about the rocks?"

"But fast rising water is the real danger," Poppy John had said. "Since the Pawpaw narrows, it doesn't take much water for the stream to overflow its bank and cover the entire pathway. If you're not careful, the rising water can quickly get you into a lot of trouble because there's no place to go. The banks are too steep to climb. That's the reason you should never go in the Pawpaw alone, Boy!"

Although Orion had paid attention to everything his grandfather told him, he had not understood much of what he had said. For example, he didn't know why the water would rise so fast. And how fast was fast? He couldn't imagine anything dangerous about the situation.

"I'm sure it has something to do with how hard it rains," he had reasoned. "But I'll just avoid the Pawpaw when it's raining, so there won't be any problem.

"Poppy John is just trying to scare me so I wouldn't find out what all the fuss is about," Orion said, as he downplayed his grandfather's warning.

Yet now he had decided he was ready to go in alone. He knew that going against his grandfather's warning about such a forbidding place would be risky. What if he found out? He didn't want to openly ignore Poppy John's authority, but the lure of proving that he could handle any situation was too powerful. It was something Orion felt he had to do.

If he had to endure this summer away from his friends and familiar surroundings, Orion decided the best way to cope with the situation was to become a daring adventurer in search of the unknown, or as he liked to think of himself, "Orion, the Courageous."

As Orion approached the Pawpaw, he closely examined the dirt road as it disappeared into a variety of shrubs, weeds, and strange looking vegetation. Majestic emerald trees lined each side of the road, with their branches forming an archway under which the road and Shannon Creek traveled together into the Pawpaw. The road, only fifteen feet wide, had once been a deer trail.

Shannon Creek was crystal clear. Huge boulders and rocks attempted to stop the water from rushing into the Pawpaw without success. Dark green moss clung to the creek's sides like a wooly overcoat. Rows of cattails stood a silent watch at the entrance.

Orion noticed there were no animals in sight, not even the frivolous chirping of birds or a squirrel's frenzied search for food. Though unusual, Orion didn't give the silence a second thought. He was much too distracted by the thought of finding out for himself why no one ever went into the Pawpaw.

Orion's mind wandered. He imagined himself in a parade, riding a bright red convertible, being showered with confetti as he waved to an adoring crowd. The huge signs that hung on overpasses and on every telephone pole especially pleased him. The signs read, "WELCOME ORION — HERO AND CONQUEROR OF THE PAWPAW."

He envisioned his mother, father, Mammaw, and Poppy John riding in a big white Cadillac, waving to the crowd while shouting alternately, "That's my boy!" and "That's my grandson!"

Being a conquering hero was something to be proud of. Making the Pawpaw safe for travel was going to be an accomplishment comparable to Daniel Boone's opening of the gateway to the West through the Cumberland Gap.

Orion suddenly remembered that conquering the Pawpaw had not yet been accomplished — and in fact, was currently being attempted without the approval of his grandfather, and that thought jolted back him to reality.

"Poppy John doesn't understand why it's important to explore unknown territory just for the thrill of it," Orion said, as he stared at the entrance.

"Too many people take the easy way out, stay close to home, and never experience the excitement of the unknown. I'll never be like that."

It was a beautiful day. As the sun started to go behind a cloud, Orion took another deep breath, looked around, and stepped into the shadows of the Pawpaw. After taking several steps, something unexpected happened — a strange feeling seized his whole body. He could not move a muscle.

Not quite sure what had him in its grip, he took several deep breaths. He started to shout for help, but concluded that it would be a waste of breath because no one was within two miles. He would save his breath because he might need it later.

Then the strange paralysis went away as quickly as it came.

Orion decided to walk back outside into the sunshine and think this over a minute. He sat down on a boulder beside the creek, still gazing intently at the opening to the Pawpaw.

He scooped up a big handful of water and splashed it on his face. The ice-cold water soothed his sweaty skin. He reached down for another handful. This time Orion let the water drip down his face to his shirt and pants. Although he had the urge to jump into the water, clothes and all, he knew he was pressed for time. Poppy John would miss him if he stayed too long.

After having a little talk with himself, Orion found his courage again and became more determined than ever to press on with his exploration.

"After all, true adventurers don't turn tail and run at the first sign of trouble," he said aloud.

He was ready to begin again his quest for safe passage through the Pawpaw. He jumped up and walked confidently to the entrance. He stopped, looked around expecting the worse, but felt nothing. He noticed for the first time that the temperature in the Pawpaw had dropped, and there was a cool breeze blowing in his face. He shivered as goose bumps covered his arms, but a little chill would not hamper his mission.

Excited and nervous at the same time, Orion started walking deeper into the Pawpaw. At first he was in no hurry because there were unusual sights to see and sounds to hear. He had gone about thirty yards when a strange, but distinctive, odor filled the air. It reminded him of entering the school gym on a hot, humid day where a bunch of kids had been sweating. His journey now had a familiarity about it.

He had walked approximately another thirty yards when the light from the entrance faded in the background, and dimness wrapped itself around him. The darkness did not faze Orion. He had long ago gotten over being afraid of the dark, but now he had a strong sensation that someone or something was nearby watching him. It was an eerie feeling — one that he had not had before. He slowly turned in a complete circle, looking for sounds and movement. A loud screech in the distance sent Orion's heart into overdrive. He jumped and screamed, "YEOOOOW!"

The Pawpaw got deathly quiet for a moment or two, and then erupted with all kinds of sounds. The noises unnerved Orion at first, but most were sounds he heard every day, like the rustling of leaves in the trees and the rushing of water. A gnawing feeling was building in his stomach. He couldn't shake the feeling that someone or something was watching his every move.

Twenty minutes later he was still walking. Suddenly, he heard raindrops hitting the canopy of leaves overhead. The rain added to the rising humidity, which made Orion sweat more. He kept wiping the moisture off with the back of his hand in order to keep his eyes open for anything that might cross his path. The rain was falling lightly, so he wasn't worried.

He was now feeling like Columbus must have felt on his unforgettable quest to find the East by sailing west. "I can't let a little rain stop me now! I have to push on!"

At times, the pathway disappeared into the creek. When it vanished, he forged ahead without worrying about wet brogans and pants. Sometimes the water was at the top of his shoes, and Orion had to be extremely careful as he made his way over slippery rocks. He concluded it would be difficult, if not impossible, to move rapidly through the creek in an emergency. He hoped there would be no emergency, but tried to prepare himself for the worst.

Several times he thought of turning around and returning the same way he had come. However, the pull of what was around the next bend was too strong.

He listened as the rain pounded the trees more rapidly. He checked the creek's level, and it looked OK for now, although it did appear to be rising. The sounds of the rain and the wind rustling through the trees became deafening.

In another twenty minutes the water was well above his shoes. This meant that the creek had risen and, without Orion noticing, the Pawpaw had narrowed significantly. He became uneasy when he suddenly felt hemmed in from all sides. He moved as fast as he could to the vegetation on the left side of the creek and picked up his pace. However, walking had become more difficult because the water was not only deeper but was moving faster as well.

As he rounded a curve, he saw a massive live oak tree fifty yards ahead on the left. "If I can make it to that tree, I'll be all right," Orion said out of desperation. "I can rest there until the water goes down."

He knew he was in deep trouble, and the fact that he was not a great swimmer made the rising water an even bigger hurdle to overcome.

Again, the uncanny feeling that someone was watching him took control of his emotions. He quickly whirled around, now expecting to see a person or — something worse. He had always heard growing up that it was not unusual for people to disappear while walking the streets of Cleveland, and he wondered if that was about to happen to him here. Maybe these thoughts were from an overactive guilty conscience for being in the Pawpaw against his grandfather's wishes. Regardless of what prompted the suspicion, Orion strongly felt that he sensed the presence of someone.

Without thinking he yelled, "Come on out! I know you're there! I can hear you!" Except for the rain, the Pawpaw was quiet.

All of a sudden, Orion stopped dead in his tracks. He had never seen such a huge tree. Each of its limbs was like another tree that reached far beyond the other bank. He noticed that its leaves were as big as a baseball glove. The trunk was large enough to put a small house inside, and he couldn't see its top.

Noises that sounded like they were coming from somewhere near the tree had gotten his attention. Orion glanced up and down the tree, but didn't see anything. He placed both hands in front of his mouth and shouted, "Who's there? Who are you? Come out and let me see you."

Suddenly, amid the whistling of the breeze, he heard something that sounded like, "Come toward the tree." But he was not absolutely sure until he distinctly heard it again: "Come toward the tree."

Orion didn't know who it was, but it was definitely a human voice. He was beside himself. He had been right: someone had followed him into the Pawpaw.

Rather than being fearful, he jumped for joy. But because he got excited, he lost his footing. Unable to regain his balance, he fell into the water and was swept away.

Orion didn't know what was happening at first, but when his head went underwater all thoughts of being "Orion, the Conqueror" left his mind. Intuitively, he recognized that he was in the fight of his life.

He could only think of reaching the bank and grabbing onto something, as he moved his arms and legs as fast as he could. But Orion was disoriented: he didn't know where the bank was — in front, beside, or behind him. That fact made him more vulnerable to the dangers of a creek out of control.

However, he tried not to panic, but after a short time he grew tired. He found it more and more difficult to move his arms and legs. He saw a bright light above him and began to move toward it by kicking his legs like he had seen frogs do many times. The frog-like movement of his legs propelled him toward the light.

Then he saw the outline of a huge figure next to the tree motioning him toward the light and shouting, "Grab my hand!"

Orion didn't know what to do as the figure continued to motion vigorously and to shout, "Orion, grab my hand! Grab my hand!"

"How does he know my name?" Orion thought, as he reached for the hand. He had difficulty grabbing it. After several attempts, he finally got it and held on for dear life. The hand was big and very strong.

It was as if he was coming out of a dream when his head was pulled out of the water. He gasped for breath with great difficulty. Then he heard someone repeatedly commanding him, "Orion, hold on! Come on! You can do it!"

"Yes, I can do it," he responded calmly. But when he tried to move, his body didn't respond. The pull of the water dragging his body down let him know he was not out of danger.

"Come on, Orion, you can make it!"

This time he seized a branch with his left hand and began to pull with all his might. With the help of the big hand, Orion made it out of the water. He was so exhausted that all he could do was to plop on the bank and lie flat on his stomach. He thought to himself: "Some conquering hero I am! Whoever saved me probably finds this whole incident quite amusing."

Through half-closed eyes, Orion saw what he thought was a bright red bandana hanging from the back pocket of a pair of overalls. The huge figure that had pulled him from the creek was walking away from him.

Orion could only manage a faint whisper, "Don't go, Poppy John!" before falling asleep, exhausted.

When Orion woke up, he had no idea how long he had been asleep. He looked around and didn't see anyone. However, the memory of the red bandana flashed before his eyes.

"Poppy John! Poppy John, where are you?" he called out.

There was no response.

His head swirled with confusion. As he worried about what sort of punishment he would face when he got home, Orion wondered, first of all, whether he should even go back home and secondly, whether his mysterious rescuer really could have been Poppy John.

"Poppy John would have stayed with me. He would have immediately made sure that I knew the consequences of disobeying him. And besides, I bet there are plenty people who wear red bandanas in their back pockets."

At this very moment, roaming the hills and creeks endlessly didn't seem so exciting. Orion felt alone, exhausted, and defeated, his idea of becoming a fearless, swashbuckling adventurer now a distant dream.

Before he attempted to stand up, he rubbed his eyes vigorously to make sure he was wide-awake. He looked around and saw footprints in the mud — his own, of course, but also a distinctly larger set leading away from the bank — which helped confirm that the whole episode had not been a dream.

He knew he had disobeyed his grandfather, which made him feel badly. Besides, Poppy John had been right: the Pawpaw was no place to be alone. A cold shiver went up his spine when it finally hit him that he had almost drowned.

As he sat and thought about everything, it sort of took Orion by surprise that it really was not the punishment he was going to get that brought such a feeling of dread inside him — it was more so the fact that he had let his grandfather down. Several weeks ago, Orion couldn't have cared less about Poppy John's feelings. He would have shrugged off the whole incident as being just a string of bad luck and would have probably had the attitude that his grandfather could take a hike if he didn't like it. But oddly enough for some reason, not now. The thought of offending Poppy John clearly upset Orion; all he could think about now was how to make up for his recklessness. But would Poppy John ever trust him again?

Orion stood up and noticed that the water level had gone down, but he decided not to finish his trek through the remainder of the Pawpaw. That would have to wait for another day.

Orion thought at that moment he should go home and confess everything to Mammaw and Poppy John as soon as possible and beg for their forgiveness. While searching for just the right words and trying to get his nerve up to tell them, he took off for the farm, still wondering what was around the next bend.

4

Getting To Know Mammaw

Sitting at the breakfast table the next morning after his dangerous journey into the Pawpaw, Orion tried to focus on the morning chores ahead, but found it difficult.

He looked up as his grandmother opened the fire door to the stove, threw in some coal, and stepped back quickly as flames shot upwards. She turned and said, "You're a million miles away this morning Orion. Want to talk about it?"

"I think I just didn't get enough sleep last night. I'll be OK as soon as I wake up," he said sleepily. For some reason, he couldn't find the courage to say what was really on his mind. It would have to wait.

Handing Orion a glass of cold milk, Mammaw said with a smile, "Here, drink this. It will help you wake up. And if it doesn't wake you up, at least it will put hair on your chest."

Orion smiled, "As the only eighth grader with a hairy chest, I certainly would be the center of attention at school, but the principal has a rule against going to class without a shirt!"

Orion stared intently at his grandmother as she laughed at his last comment. She was in no way fancy, but Orion thought she was still pretty in her own way, especially when she smiled. Her shoulder-length gray hair she usually had pinned up in the back, and she always wore a long cotton dress — today it was the blue gingham-checked one. She was a small woman with strong hands that moved heavy pots or lifted buckets of coal with ease. Her hands reflected a life of hard work. Calluses, wrinkles, and age spots had long since replaced the softness and beauty of youth, yet her hands were as delicate as a baby's when she hugged Orion and tenderly stroked his cheek.

Orion watched as his grandmother glided gracefully from stove to table and back to the stove humming the same tune over and over. Orion wondered if she had ever wanted to be a ballet dancer — her movements were so smooth and effortless.

The kitchen was Mammaw's exclusive territory. Poppy John didn't ramble around in the kitchen as he did in other rooms. The only time Orion saw his grandfather in the kitchen was at meal times. Then when Poppy John finished eating, he immediately went to the front porch to smoke.

Orion couldn't help but admire his grandmother because he felt she was genuine — that is, she said what she meant and meant what she said. She had overcome a lot in her life, not the least of which had been raising ten children. Orion felt that he had known her all his life and talking to her came naturally.

Mammaw frequently turned to Orion during these morning sessions and gave him a wink and a big smile. When he wasn't paying attention, she would sneak up on him, give him a big hug, toss his hair and teasingly exclaim, "You should give me that red hair! It's too pretty for a boy!" Then she would laugh loudly and go back to cooking.

He enjoyed being in the kitchen with his grandmother and often pretended not to be paying attention just to get a hug.

"Mammaw, what's for breakfast?" Orion would always ask, as if he didn't know.

"Well, let me see. Let's have those fried apples you love so much, and then we'll throw in biscuits, eggs, sausage, bacon, fried potatoes and gravy. We'll end our breakfast adventure with the Saddler specialty: homemade blackberry jelly. So save some room!"

Orion always closed his eyes and smiled as his grandmother recited the morning's menu, which didn't change much from morning to morning. The aromas, however, seemed to get better each morning. This morning's dominant smell was bacon frying — crisp, delightful bacon.

Another aroma that pleased Orion was that of fried apples. Orion loved the way Mammaw topped his with a sprinkle of cinnamon-sugar.

And there was nothing he liked better than fried apples, unless it was when his grandmother rolled the apple slices in dough, fried them, and sang, "Apple Pan Dowdy makes your eyes light up and your tummy say howdy..." Mammaw made Apple Pan Dowdies so light they melted in his mouth. Orion liked to get a mouthful, close his eyes, and savor their taste for several seconds before he started chewing.

He recalled the first morning that his grandmother served him fried apples. Concerned that he might not like the taste, Orion had asked, "Apples? I didn't know you could fry them. I mean, apples are apples, and I like them just the way they come, right off the tree!"

Mammaw had reassured him that fried apples had a special flavor and texture and that the only problem was, "once you taste them, you might never eat a raw apple again."

Mammaw persuaded Orion to give them a try, promising she'd never bother him about it again if he didn't like them. After the first mouthful, he smiled and said, "Keep the apples coming, Mammaw. They're delicious!"

One morning while his grandmother was making apple fritters, Orion asked, "Why don't you use more store-bought food?"

Mammaw turned around, smiled, and said, "We grow most everything we need, and what we don't grow we trade for at the Gap store. Take these apples, for example — we not only eat them ourselves, but we trade a few bushels at the Gap each fall for animal feed."

As far as Orion ever knew before, everything that a person needed to eat was bought at a grocery store. Trading food for other foods or goods was new to Orion.

Mammaw explained that by placing bushels of apples in an earthen storeroom dug into the mountain, they were able to have fresh apples all winter. The storeroom was like a refrigerator, and it kept a variety of foods fresh and cool for months.

Orion found out later that his grandparents had little money for store-bought items. Animal feed and Poppy John's smoking papers were among the few items routinely bought. Occasionally, Mammaw would get cloth for a dress or for a shirt for Poppy John. He couldn't imagine Poppy John doing without rolling papers for his cigarettes, so Orion was careful not to ask for anything that had to be bought.

While Orion admired his grandmother, she had one annoying habit that he didn't understand — smoking a pipe. A blackened corncob pipe was her favorite. She carried a faded Prince Albert can refilled with Poppy John's tobacco with her everywhere she went; it was tied with a string around her waist, so it bounced as she walked.

When Orion had asked why she smoked a pipe, Mammaw told him, "Old Doc Millford told me to smoke for medical reasons. Of course, he didn't tell me what those medical reasons were. Come to think of it, I liked the tobacco so much, I never did ask him," she added with a wink.

Orion remembered learning in school that at one time it was thought that smoking tobacco was good for your health. He wondered if he should bring up the scientific facts he'd been taught, about how dangerous it actually is.

"Maybe another day, when I get my courage up," Orion decided.

Poppy John usually had a cigarette in his hand. Tobacco was like most things on the farm — homegrown. Poppy John grew it on a small plot at the back of the house, then hung it up in a small shed to dry. He bought Prince Albert cigarette papers onto which he poured the tobacco, and then hand-rolled each cigarette with great care. He smoked each cigarette until the tobacco was almost gone; consequently, a dark, permanent stain adorned several fingers on his right hand.

Poppy John always smelled of stale tobacco, and Orion wanted to avoid that unpleasant stench at all costs. Orion decided early that smoking was a nasty habit, and that he wanted no part of it. Being around it all the time now just confirmed what he'd already decided.

Mammaw asked, "What are you doing today, Orion? Anything exciting?"

"Not really. I may go fishing when it gets hot, or I may get Elvin to show me some new blackberry patches."

"If you go to Shannon Creek, be careful of crawdads. They should be out in droves today. If you go blackberry picking, bring back enough for a pie."

"Oh, yes, Mammaw! I just put blackberry hunting at the top of my list of things to do today," Orion replied, grinning from ear to ear, as the image of Mammaw's warm blackberry pie with homemade ice cream made his tummy growl.

Orion knew he had chores to do that would take up most of the morning, so after eating as much as he could, Orion got up from the table and expressed his appreciation to Mammaw: "Thank you for a wonderful breakfast; I've never had better."

"Oh, hush!" Mammaw teased. "You're saying that just to make me blush."

They laughed and gave each other a big hug.

For a split second, Orion thought about crawling back into the warmth of the featherbed and taking a long nap, but he knew the hungry animals needed food now.

He hummed as he walked to the chicken coop. Orion felt so carefree that he started talking to the chickens: "Today is going to be a great day, ladies! Eat up, so you can cluck another day!" Talking to chickens was something Orion did not usually do.

This morning Orion kept thinking about Mammaw, that she was the most gentle and caring person he had ever met. She never raised her voice in anger, even at the dogs the day they ate a freshly baked gingerbread stack cake that had been set out to cool. She had only commented, "They must have really been hungry," and immediately started making another cake.

Mammaw was patient with Orion and understood that he had a

lot to learn about the farm. However, she didn't have to worry about his willingness to try his hand at farm work. Orion was eager to learn, and he didn't goof off when there was work to be done. She was very pleased with Orion's progress and told him so often.

Orion thought about when he first had arrived at the farm, how he had never heard of, let alone eaten, poke salad. Mammaw took care of that in a hurry. One day she motioned and said, "Come on, Orion! Let's go pick some poke salad." He was game for anything, especially if it meant spending time with his grandmother.

"What in the world is poke salad?" he asked. Orion had visions of some type of icky stuff hanging from trees, but he was in for a surprise.

"Poke salad is like lettuce but much greener, and the leaves are larger. We eat it as a cooked vegetable or a salad," Mammaw replied.

After walking a mile, they came to a large clearing. Mammaw stopped, pointed to a field ahead, and said with a laugh, "There it is: Poke Salad Alley." Orion saw many kinds of grasses, weeds, and leafy green plants, and asked, "Where's the poke?"

She pointed out a leafy, green plant with reddish stalks and said, "There you are — poke salad."

Mammaw showed him how to pick the smaller leaves, leaving the largest plants with dark purple berries alone. "The young, tender leaves have the mildest flavor," she told Orion.

Orion and Mammaw would go to Poke Salad Alley about twice a week to gather the abundant green plant. At first Orion didn't like the taste, but he learned to love it when Mammaw poured generous amounts of hot bacon grease and bits on top of it.

Orion got to see a special side of his grandmother on the poke salad outings. She was full of practical advice about the farm, and she had an unusual sense of humor that went over Orion's head at first. Initially it was difficult for Orion to talk about personal things, but as he got to know his grandmother better, he could talk about anything that was on his mind — even girls.

"I've been wanting to walk Becky Lou Smith home from school for a long time," Orion blurted out one afternoon. "I've always been afraid to ask her, but I think I've got my nerve up now. First day of school, I'm going to ask her!"

He talked about his shyness, and how he would sometimes act out just to get attention. Although shy, Orion didn't want to be ignored.

One day Orion asked, "How will I know when I meet the girl I should marry?"

Mammaw replied, "You're a little young to worry about marrying, but one thing's sure — there will be many girls who will tug at your heart, but only one will win it."

Orion playfully responded, "Oh, Mammaw! I'll never give my heart to anyone but you."

Mammaw slapped her knee and declared with a hearty laugh, "You are the sweetest talking boy this side of the Mississippi River. You'll never have any problem getting pretty girls to walk by your side!"

She thought for a minute, then continued: "A person never knows when the love of a lifetime will walk through the door. It's funny. You never quite know when it's going to happen, but when it does you know it right away. Then you get all silly and fall all over yourself. Even if you're the best talker in the whole world, your tongue gets tied, and you can't think of anything to say."

Orion shrugged his shoulders, and said, "If my dream girl walks through the door, I hope my mouth doesn't blurt out something stupid, or she'll walk on by to someone else's door!"

Both of them smiled and kept on walking.

On one poke salad outing, Mammaw shared a wish of her own: "Orion, I'll tell you a secret — I'd like to see the ocean before I die. People say there's nothing but water as far as the eye can see and ships as big as mountains."

Orion noticed her eyes were getting moist with tears as she talked. Then she said, "Oh, well, we've got better things to do today than to talk about a big old ocean! Come on, Orion, we've got to pick some poke salad for supper."

Orion assured her that she would see the ocean some day, and maybe even ride on a big ship. Mammaw just smiled and said, "Perhaps, perhaps."

Those words stuck with Orion for the rest of the summer, and secretly he vowed to help Mammaw see the ocean somehow, some-day.

5

Buying A Ten Dollar Pig

Orion stepped off the front porch, sighed, and took in a deep breath of fresh morning air. It was a morning like any other: a crisp breeze had blown in from the southeast, and the fragrant smell of honeysuckle had seeped into every nook and corner of Saddler Mountain. He felt like beating his chest and yelling like Tarzan, but he thought better of it.

Orion looked forward to taking in the sights, sounds, and smells in the stillness of early morning. "Today is going to be a great day," he thought. But unknown to Orion, events were already underway to make the day a memorable one, if not a great one.

Orion always fed the chickens first because it didn't take long. He returned several times during the day to make sure they had enough water. He usually collected the eggs on his second trip to the coop.

The food had to be distributed evenly over the entire chicken yard because Poppy John said it was important for them to move around as they ate. And move they did — pecking nonstop, hour after hour, every few seconds letting out a loud cluck, cluck, cluck.

Orion enjoyed seeing the chickens scamper for the food as he rhythmically called out in a higher-pitched tone of voice: "Chick, chick, chick, chick — here, chick; here, chick." Some days when he was feeling really good, he sang his own version of the Old McDonald song: "Here a chick, there a chick, everywhere a chick, chick. Old McOrion had some chicks, E-I-E-I-O!"

This morning, he watched attentively as the chickens attacked the crushed corn with zeal. "What a life. I should be so lucky," he observed. "It would be neat to eat all day long without a care in the world."

Actually the chickens did have one worry: Mammaw. She was the official chicken neck-wringer, so when they heard her sing out sweetly, "Here chick, here chick," they all ran like crazy. Mammaw knew how to make the unpleasant task of transforming them into Sunday's main course as quick and nearly painless as possible, by giving the unfortunate birds a simple jerk of the neck, then plucking their feathers in scalding water, and cleaning them out. Then she cut up the pieces, rolled them in a mixture of flour and just the right spices, and fried them in a hot iron skillet.

Chickens amused Orion for several reasons. First, they were funny looking — with no teeth or lips — and second, they were not very smart. Being short of brainpower made chickens vulnerable to every danger that came along. For example, rather than running when a snake came close, a chicken moved closer to get a better look. Talk about dumb! But their lack of caution was not surprising since they had a brain about the size of a pea.

When hens laid eggs, their pea brains went into overdrive. They would cackle and cackle their little hearts out and strut all over the hen house, with their heads moving back and forth. It was as if each chicken had given the world the long-awaited golden egg.

Rojo casually observed the Sunday neck-wringing ritual, but it never seemed to ruffle his feathers. Perhaps he sensed that he would never occupy the bottom of a frying pan. When Orion asked his grandmother why she never went after the rooster, she simply said, "Roosters are tough old birds. The only thing they're good for is strutting in front of the hens." Although Orion didn't understand the significance of Rojo strutting to and fro in front of the hens, he laughed heartily as he commented, "I certainly agree that he is good for nothing!"

Orion's first reaction to the neck-wringing was one of revulsion, but as time went on he viewed it as necessary. He accepted it as part of living on a farm; after all, there were no grocery markets to buy chicken already prepared for cooking. And besides, he loved Mammaw's southern fried chicken.

Mammaw planned the Sunday menu months in advance, since she knew which chicken would mature at just the right time for the best taste. After a brief flurry of scampering and loud clucking by the chickens, everything was back to normal. The remaining chickens resumed their endless pecking as if nothing had happened.

Orion made a special effort not to get too friendly with any of the chickens. He avoided naming them like he did the rest of the farm animals because he couldn't stand the thought of having a friend for dinner. The chickens didn't seem to mind anyway, since they mostly ignored him.

After feeding the chickens, Orion headed back to the kitchen to pick up leftovers for the pigs. A variety of food scraps left over from previous meals was always available, including biscuits, cornbread, vegetables of one sort or another, and gravy. Since coming to the farm, he discovered that his grandparents never threw food away. If food was left at a meal, it was saved for the next meal, or until the next round of feeding the dogs and pigs.

This particular morning there was a half-bucket of leftovers from last night's supper and this morning's breakfast. Orion mixed the table scraps with water, oats, corn, and other grains before taking it to the pigpen. Orion got ten ears of dried corn each morning from the corncrib and shucked them into the large bucket. He stuffed several whole ears of corn into his pants as rewards for the pigs.

Poppy John called the mixture "slop" and dubbed the feeding of the pigs, "slopping the hogs." Orion couldn't force himself to say "slop," because it had such an unpleasant sound to it.

The food smelled terrible, as did the pigpen itself, and he had to tell himself, "At least, I don't have to eat it." However, the pigs were all alike when it came to slop — they couldn't get enough of it.

Besides feeding the animals and making sure they had enough water throughout the day, cleaning the barn and pigpen rounded out the daily list of chores for Orion. The cleaning of the pigpen proved more unpleasant than any of the other chores.

"Cleaning up after the pigs is the honey dipper patrol," Poppy John had said on Orion's first day at the farm.

"You'll soon find out why the honey dipper patrol is such a terrific task."

Orion had said, sarcastically, "I can hardly wait to find out."

Farm animals, especially pigs, are not sanitary. They dispose of their bodily waste whenever and wherever they feel like it. Cleaning the pigpen — or as Poppy John affectionately called it, the honey dipper patrol — was sheer drudgery. It didn't take Orion long to realize that the animal waste was the "honey," he was the "dipper," and he had to patrol the pigpen constantly to stay ahead of the waste.

At first Orion thought the pigs deposited their waste on purpose just to make him mad, so he ridiculed them for their lack of cleanliness. He would yell, "Nasty oinkers!" when they dirtied the area after he had cleaned it, but discovered verbal taunts and name-calling were useless. They continued to make a mess, and Orion repeatedly had to clean up after them.

The aroma was definitely not like that of honey — for the first week Orion had to wear a handkerchief over his nose and mouth. Yet nothing could keep out the disgusting smell. To his amazement, however, he soon got used to the foul odor.

Orion declared that the pigs would watch every move he made, snorting loudly if he didn't clean every inch of the pen. He would test them by leaving a small area unclean, and then address them mockingly, "Let's see you catch this one today, you picky oinkers!" It became a test of wills — Orion's versus the pigs'. Orion was at a distinct disadvantage.

Even though he tried every trick in the book to outwit them, nothing worked. Finally his grandfather said, "There's no outsmarting those pigs, Boy. They are smart enough to know you're playing with them, and they like the game."

It was difficult for Orion to admit, but Poppy John was right — the pigs always caught his attempts at trickery.

Working on the farm definitely required a bath every night, something Orion was not used to. But as he was walking to the house after the first day's chores, he smelled something foul in the air. Attempting to pinpoint its source, he turned around quickly expecting to find the animals lined up behind him. They were not, yet the scent persisted. After ten minutes of looking all around him, Orion realized that the barnyard odor had invaded every pore and cavity of his body and clothes. He smelled like the pigpen.

"Yuck!" he yelled, as he headed toward the stream as fast as he could run. He jumped in without taking his clothes off, and spent the next fifteen minutes in the water scrubbing with leaves and sand. Only the dinner bell drove him from the water.

Bathing in the stream quickly became a daily ritual. When Orion bathed, the goat, horse, cows, ducks, and dogs (when they were around) seemed to crowd around to watch. Even the pigs lined up against their fence, snorting and acting silly. Orion never got used to their prying eyes; he told Mammaw he always felt like a goldfish in a bowl. He would scream and splash water at them, but there was no discouraging them.

He ventured a guess as to why they enjoyed watching him so much — "Since they never take a bath, they must not understand using water for anything other than drinking."

Orion named what would become his favorite pig "Charlene," on the first day he saw her. Charlene Bell was the older sister of one of his friends who always shouted at them to go play somewhere else. Needless to say, Orion thought she was a smart aleck, so when he named the pig Charlene he laughed at the prospect of turning the tables on her. He would have a great time ordering Charlene around for a change. But he became rather fond of the name as his attachment to the pig grew. Charlene turned out to be the smartest and most loving animal on the farm. Any idea of harassing Charlene soon went out the window.

Although cleaning up after them was the worst job, Orion loved to feed the pigs because they were so grateful, wagging their tails and squealing with delight when they saw him. Charlene was always by the fence, eager for him to arrive. Although she loved to eat, Charlene waited for Orion because she craved the attention he gave her. She would not eat a bite of food until he had given her a big hug. There were many mornings Orion had to hug her after she had wallowed in the mud. But after he got used to it, he didn't mind because it was easy to wash off in the creek.

After eating, Charlene loved to play tag. She would hit Orion in the leg with her snout, and then run with her curly tail wagging wildly. When Orion got close, she would squeal as loud as she could. You'd think someone was after her with a butcher knife! He would chase her around the pen until he caught her, sometimes in the mud. It was not always clear which one caught the other. Charlene was a tough tag opponent because she could run fast, could stop on a dime, and was very slippery when wet.

The game went on until Orion got too tired to run, and he would plop down in the grass. Charlene would go back to the feeding trough to finish eating.

During these brief rests, Orion would gaze at the clouds moving across the sky. He liked to identify their shapes — cars, trains, ships, dogs, sheep, chickens, and cows — as they passed by overhead on their way to who knows where. He imagined that Indian chiefs on magnificent horses often rode across the sky, on their way to the Happy Hunting Ground.

Orion regretted not ever having seen a cloud that looked like a giraffe. He told himself that perhaps giraffes could only be seen in clouds over Africa.

Orion thought giraffes were the most beautiful animals in the world. His fifth grade teacher, Ms. Greisch, had assigned a research paper, and Orion had chosen to write about giraffes. The giraffe project had been the last time Orion had taken school seriously.

He shared what he knew about giraffes with Charlene several times. She seemed to be interested, and the sessions provided Orion an opportunity to show off his considerable knowledge of giraffes.

Charlene always listened when Orion talked, and she would wait for a lull in the conversation to grunt knowingly. Orion appreciated the companionship.

Once Orion established the routine with Charlene and the other pigs, the feeding process went smoothly — until today. It would be a day firmly etched in Orion's memory.

When he arrived at the pigpen, the pigs were full of nervous energy, as if waiting for something to happen. Charlene was at her usual place biding her time anxiously.

Attempting to coax a little life from the group, Orion banged on the bucket and said, "Come on guys! The food is extra delicious this morning — lots of biscuits and gravy. Yum, yum, yum." Other than a half-hearted grunt from Charlene, there was no response. He sang in an attempt to get them in a better mood, but that didn't work either.

He then hugged Charlene, and tried to encourage her, "What's wrong, girl? Are you feeling bad? Come on, I'll rub your belly after you eat. That will make you feel better." He then walked to a corner of the pen to wait for Charlene.

Charlene nibbled at her food, but it didn't take long for her to eat all she wanted. As she started toward Orion, she suddenly squealed and ran past him on her way to the far side of the pen. He knew something was wrong because the squeal had the sound of terror. Soon there was total chaos in the pigpen. Pigs ran in every direction, squealing as loud as they could. At first, Orion thought the black panther might have gotten past the dogs, but then he saw Poppy John coming straight for the pen. His grandfather was carrying a large sledgehammer over his shoulder.

Orion jumped up and ran to the fence, calling out, "Poppy John, what are you doing with that big hammer? What's broken? Can I help?"

Poppy John didn't respond immediately; he kept his eyes on the pigs. He stopped next to Orion and said, "Nothing's broken, Boy, but we've got some serious business to attend to."

"Serious business?"

"We need more summer feed for the animals, and selling pork is the only way to get it."

It didn't immediately register with Orion that Poppy John had brought the hammer to use on one of the pigs. He knew that bacon and pork chops came from pigs, but how the meat got from the pigpen to the table was something he had never thought about.

Poppy John handed the hammer to Orion and said, "Hold this while I climb over the fence."

The hammer was so heavy that Orion almost dropped it, but he managed to get a grip on it. Before Poppy John started over the fence, Mammaw called out, "Poppy John, you promised to move the kitchen table before you went to the pen."

Poppy John replied, "OK, Mammaw, in a minute." He looked at Orion as he started toward the house, and said, "Remember: pigs are not pets. They're here to provide food for us and, occasionally, for our neighbors."

As Poppy John's words sank in, Orion asked softly, "Why would you kill animals for food?" but Poppy John was already out of hearing range. Once the words passed his lips, he knew it was a stupid question.

"I just won't eat any meat," he blurted out, "that will show them!" A few moments later, he said to himself, "Boy, how stupid!" It was stupid because, whether he ate meat or not, the pigs would still be killed. He also thought of all the delicious chicken, ham, pork chops, bacon, and sausage he had already eaten for the past two months.

"Of course," he consoled himself, "but that was before I knew the whole story." Then it hit him, "What if Poppy John's after Charlene?"

Orion's mind became a nonstop machine, searching for a way to save Charlene. "But what can I do? Poppy John and Mammaw have to eat. Maybe they can become vegetarians! No, even I don't like the idea of eating just vegetables. And besides, they're too old to change their ways. I know: I'll go home — that way I won't have to be a part of this whole mess. But what good would that do? Charlene would still be done in. I don't have a car, and it's too far to walk. OK then, how about killing only chickens — they're useless anyway. Chickens are delicious; everyone loves fried chicken!"

By now, Orion was really nervous. He realized killing animals for food was perhaps necessary. But he didn't have time to consider the matter further because Poppy John was on his way back to the pigpen. He decided that if he couldn't free all the animals, he would at least try to save Charlene.

As Poppy John approached, Orion pleaded, "You can't hit Charlene! Please, Poppy John, don't kill Charlene!"

His grandfather reached for the hammer, looked Orion in the eyes and said, "Boy, I know this is hard for you since it's your first time, but this is why we raise pigs."

"But Charlene is my pet!" Orion pleaded, almost in tears. He couldn't imagine Charlene as a pork chop.

Poppy John paused, and said, "I'm not after Charlene today. But remember, Boy, this is how we survive."

Orion was relieved that Charlene wasn't getting clobbered, but that meant her day would eventually come. He thought a hammer was a cruel way to put an end to a pig's life, so he asked his grandfather, "Why do you use a hammer? There must be a nicer way."

"Boy, there isn't a nice way to kill a pig. If you have to kill an animal, then the hammer is the best way. When I hit a pig between the eyes with this hammer, it doesn't have time to feel a thing. It's all over in a second."

Orion remained silent, but thought, "One day Charlene will be staring down the long handle of the hammer, and that makes me sick."

Time was running out. He had to think of something. Just as Orion was about to concede defeat, he blurted out, "I want to buy Charlene!"

Poppy John stopped in his tracks and said, "Buy Charlene! What on earth for?"

"I want her for my very own — as a pet," said a freshly inspired Orion.

"A pet? Who ever heard of a pet pig?"

Orion shot right back, "There's always a first time."

"But you can't take her home with you."

"I'll pay you to take care of her when I'm not here."

"You don't have any money."

"I've got some money saved at home! How much will it take to buy her?"

"Oh, about ten dollars — that's a special deal just for you," Poppy John answered.

"OK, I'll give you ten dollars for her."

"Your father won't like you spending your money on a pig."

"Maybe. But it's my money. I earned it, and Charlene is not just a pig — she's my friend. I can always make more money, but there will never be another Charlene."

Poppy John thought for a moment. He respected Orion's determination to buy Charlene, and he knew that as far as Orion was concerned, there would never be another one quite like her. He gave Orion a quick look and said, "I guess you're right about Charlene. She's not just any old pig."

He put his hand to his chin and said, "OK, I'll tell you what I'll do, I'll sell Charlene to you for ten dollars. You can send me the money when you get back home."

Orion didn't hesitate as he shouted, "Deal!" and grabbed his grandfather's hand. He immediately jumped the fence, ran over to Charlene, and gave her a big hug.

Amid Orion's sudden burst of joy, Poppy John said, "Boy, you may not want to watch this," as he moved toward a huge pig, the one Orion had named Goliath, the Gentle Giant.

"You're right. I'll go on over to the barn and take Prince for a walk." He turned, jumped over the fence, and headed for the barn. He did not look back. Just as he got to the big sycamore tree in the front yard he heard a loud "THUD," and then a loud scream, "Get away, you beast!"

Orion turned and saw Poppy John running for his life with

Goliath in hot pursuit. This time, however, the pig was not in a gentle mood. He was angry and squealing as loud as he could. Orion couldn't tell who was yelling the loudest, Poppy John or Goliath.

Just as Poppy John started to climb the fence, Goliath bit him hard on the back of his leg. Poppy John yelled louder than any rooster ever thought about crowing, and cried out, "Get this pig off me!"

By that time Orion was at the fence shouting, "Let go!" as he slapped Goliath on the snout. Goliath backed off, paused, and then rammed his head into Poppy John's rear end to remind him of the seriousness with which he took being hit in the head with a sledgehammer.

"No!" Orion said loudly. It was only then that Goliath retreated, with Poppy John falling hard on the ground.

Orion didn't know whether to laugh or cry. On the one hand, it was funny seeing his grandfather trying to outrun a three-hundred-pound pig in what turned out to be an unfair advantage for the pig. On the other hand, Poppy John's leg was bleeding from the bite.

"Help me get to the house to take care of this," Poppy John said.

"Yes, sir." Orion agreed, hardly able to hold back laughing. "What happened?"

Poppy John was obviously agitated, but answered, "I hit that pig squarely between the eyes, and he stood there with a funny look on his face — not moving or making a sound. Then he shook his head and took out after me. That pig has the hardest head on earth!"

Orion tried to be kind, but he was having a hard time sympathizing with his grandfather's attempt to carry out what he had earlier called "serious business."

After Poppy John had gone back to the house, Orion returned to the pen to celebrate Charlene's freedom. He jumped around, acted silly, and giggled until his side hurt. When Prince came out of the barn to see what the fuss was about, Orion ran over and gave him a big hug. As usual, Prince shrugged it off as just another human quirk and went back inside the barn.

Orion felt good about himself for having saved his "friend's" life.

He thought that buying Charlene was probably the best investment he would ever make.

6
Entering The Saddler Coalmine

The Saddler coalmine provided fuel for the kitchen stove and two fireplaces, one in the living room and one in the big bedroom. A fire burned in the kitchen stove every day, as did the two fireplaces in late fall, winter, and early spring. Sustaining a fire for cooking and warmth took a large amount of coal that had to be dug by hand and carried from the coalmine to the house.

The mineshaft penetrated Saddler Mountain for a half-mile. The mine was in disrepair because Poppy John had neither the equipment nor the time to keep it in good shape. There were huge blocks of slate that partially blocked the entrance. Similar chunks of slate weighing as much as two tons were scattered along the pathway to where the coal was dug. It was not a safe environment.

Poppy John dug coal three times a week during the spring, summer, and fall; most days he could complete digging and carrying the coal to the house in two hours. On some days, especially during cooler weather in late fall, he would have to make two trips. The coal buckets were heavy, and he had to rest on his return trip to the house.

During the winter, Poppy John would hitch up Prince to a big wooden wagon, fill it with coal, and make the difficult haul through snow, rain, and sleet. It usually took him the entire day to get enough coal for the week. Once Poppy John completed the laborious task, he pulled his favorite chair close to the living room fire and took a much-deserved rest.

Although a critical farm resource, the mine had major drawbacks: it was always dark, damp, and dangerous. Though Poppy John entered the mine warm, dry, and clean, he came out wet, cold, and dirty.

Orion often watched his grandfather wash the black coal dust off when he got to the house. Although it was a dirty, backbreaking, time-consuming job, Orion never heard his grandfather complain about the effort it took to keep the fires burning.

One day Orion asked his grandfather, "Can I go into the mine with you tomorrow?"

"No way, Boy," Poppy John immediately replied. "Why would you want to go into the mine?"

His grandfather's pointed response startled him, but Orion responded calmly, "I've never been inside one before, and this may be my only chance to explore a real coalmine."

"Well, that's not a good reason to go into that dangerous black dungeon!"

Orion had to think quickly, "OK, but what if your back goes out, and Mammaw needs coal to keep the fires burning? Who would get the coal? I wouldn't know what to do, and the neighbors are too far away to help immediately."

Poppy John fell silent for a moment and then said, "That's a good point, Boy. You would need to know how to get coal. OK, I'll tell you what — you can come with me on one condition: this will be your one and only journey into the mine, other than in an emergency."

Poppy John extended his hand as Orion shook it, smiled, and answered, "Yes, sir."

Orion didn't think going inside a coalmine was a big deal, until he and his grandfather entered the Saddler mine the next day. After only a few feet inside, Orion stopped suddenly because the light had faded so fast. A wall of pure darkness stared him in the face. Orion thought maybe he had made a mistake by making such a fuss about going into the mine, but this was not the time to chicken out. After all, it was his idea.

"Is it always this cold in the mine?" Orion asked nervously.

"Yes. It's always the same temperature inside."

"How can that be?"

"Well, since the usual things that make temperatures go up and down — sun, wind, rain, and snow — do not make their way into the mine, the temperature remains the same. The air, however, gets staler, colder, and thinner as we go deeper into the mine, so we can't stay too long."

The thought of breathing stale air did not set well with Orion. Poppy John hadn't mentioned the lack of fresh air in previous conversations. Orion had been so anxious to explore the coalmine that he forgot to ask any questions that he would later find out were important.

Because Poppy John didn't have a flashlight, he placed an old hard hat with a carbide lamp on Orion's head. The lamp would provide the only light they would have to make their way to the coal. Orion soon realized that the amount of flame produced by the lamp was very small.

The burning carbide smelled like rotten eggs. The odor made him gag at first, but he soon got used to it.

Just when the two advanced to a point where the outside light had faded completely, the carbide flame flickered and went out. Total darkness enveloped them. Fear immediately gripped Orion.

Poppy John immediately said, "Don't move. I'll light it."

As Orion stood still, he heard tiny squeaks and what sounded like tiny feet running around. He reached frantically for Poppy John and asked, "What's that?"

His grandfather struck a match, and then Orion saw them. "Rats!" he shrieked.

As Poppy John lit the lamp, he said, "Yes, but don't worry — they won't harm you."

"Don't worry? What if I step on one?"

"They don't take too kindly to that, so be careful where you step."

"Are there any more surprises that I should be aware of?" Orion asked cautiously.

"Like what?"

"Like flesh-eating monsters that just happen to love total darkness and attack people wandering around in this gloomy place!"

"Oh, no!" Poppy John replied, with a laugh. "Nothing like that, but there are bats, though."

"Bats! And I suppose they're really vampires that sneak out at night to attack unsuspecting prey. I bet they grow to enormous lengths here in the dark."

"Actually, they're rather timid, and I've never seen one bigger than six inches. Of course that doesn't mean that larger ones don't exist somewhere in here," Poppy John answered, chuckling. "Don't worry. The bats are more afraid of you than you are of them, and they can see you in the dark with radar. You'll be fine."

"Oh, great! Now I not only have to worry about filthy rats gnawing at my feet, but other creepy creatures of the dark landing on my head. I won't know whether to jump or duck!"

Poppy John didn't respond, but moved on ahead.

Orion stuck close to Poppy John for the rest of the trip. He heard an occasional flapping of wings, but the sounds were always ahead of or behind them.

He didn't see any rats again, but he heard them scurrying all around him. There must have been hundreds. It finally occurred to Orion that he was not the object of the rats' attention. They were concerned with only one objective — gathering food.

Making sure he didn't step on a rat took much concentration. The focus on the rats momentarily took his attention away from the growing feeling that his idea of exploring a coalmine for fun was a stupid thing to do.

The deeper they went into the mine, the more the air became colder and mustier, just as Poppy John had predicted. The stale air made Orion's breathing heavier. The last twenty yards, they had to crawl on their knees because the space suddenly narrowed to only four feet high. By the time they reached the coal, Orion had completely forgotten about rats and bats — his top priority had become regaining his normal breathing and somehow keeping warm.

In order for the lamp to provide enough light for Poppy John to dig and load coal into the buckets, Orion had to get close to him without getting hit by the pickax. Being this close to the pickax made Orion uneasy. Because he was shivering from being wet and cold, he had difficulty holding the lamp steady. He finally had to take it off his head and hold it in his hand.

"Hold on for a few more minutes; I'm almost finished," Poppy John said, sensing Orion's uneasiness.

"OK."

Orion had never been this close to passing out in his entire life. Rats, bats, darkness, stale air, and being wet and cold were more than he had bargained for.

Finally he heard his grandfather say, "Come on, Boy, it's time to go."

It was the best invitation Orion had ever received. Poppy John didn't have to tell him again because Orion was moving before the last word was spoken.

The trip out of the mine was much faster than going in, even with Poppy John dragging the coal buckets. When Orion caught his first glimpse of the entrance, he yelled, "Hurrah! There's the light!" and headed in its direction. Both he and Poppy John laughed, but Orion was deadly serious about getting out as fast as he could.

Orion kissed the ground when he got out of the mine, took several deep breaths of fresh air, and stretched his arms toward the sky. "This is more like it!" he shouted, as if he wanted to tell the whole world. There would be no more exploratory trips into the coalmine for Orion — for any reason.

That evening Orion sat on the front porch in a serious mood. The experience inside the coalmine sent his emotions on a downward spiral. He had bathed twice to get the stench of the mine off his skin. As he heard the rustling of the wind through the trees, his mind settled down. The sights, sounds, and smells of the night kept his attention.

Orion spent many evenings on the front porch. The time on the porch started as a way to cool down after his grandparents went to bed. However, it soon became a time when Orion could explore the thoughts and questions that had come up during the day without having to worry about putting the wellbeing of the animals first. The questions helped him to see that life was full of possibilities.

The porch was the best place to think about important issues because it was quiet, and he didn't have to come up with the correct answers. The time also helped him to inquire deeply into his own personal views about right and wrong. He struggled time and again about the subject of raising animals for food, and he finally decided it was OK — as long as it wasn't Charlene.

He enjoyed opening his senses to the night. There was something about the night that fueled his imagination. He became a very good listener by focusing attention on the many sounds of the evening. Over time, it became easy to pick out the distinct sounds of the various species of owls, frogs, cicadas, and crickets, besides hearing the occasional quack of a duck, moo of a cow, grunt of a pig, or neigh from Prince. Other sounds were more unusual and unfamiliar — and unsettling to his nerves. Yet all the sounds together became nature's symphony when Orion sat back and let the music of the night take hold of him.

Some nights, he would take long walks to check on Charlene or Prince, and then spend time by Shannon Creek. The running water seemed to make a different sound at night than it did during the day. The stillness of the night calmed and relaxed him, and he came back from those walks ready for a sound night's sleep.

Orion hummed "Home on the Range" on this particular evening as he sat and took in the sights and sounds. When he got to the end, he thought to himself, "Yeah, that's true — I never hear a discouraging word around here."

Before going in, Orion took one last look in the direction of Shannon Creek and saw a shooting star. He gasped, as he thought, "For a day that started out so badly, it sure ended with a bang."

He made a wish and went to bed.

7
Searching For Blackberries

Orion woke the next morning with a strong craving for Saddler Mountain's wild delicacy — the scrumptious blackberry. That meant he would spend most of the day with Elvin, the one-eyed goat. With a little luck, by hurrying through his chores, he would be on the hunt by ten o'clock and home by three in time for an afternoon swim.

Some of the fearful emotions from his unpleasant experience in the coalmine yesterday lingered, but a handful or two of perfectly ripe, plump, sweet blackberries was just the remedy to help him forget all about it. Elvin had an instinctive knack for finding every blackberry patch within three miles of the farm and seemed to know just when the blackberries ripened in each one. Orion was grateful for Elvin's special talent because he could always eat as many blackberries as he could get his hands on.

Sometimes Mammaw would send them for out to pick blackberries just so she could make Orion's favorite — blackberry pie.

"Orion, get that goofy one-eyed goat and go pick some berries. We're having blackberry pie!" she would say with a gleam in her eye.

Mammaw always fixed dessert on Sunday. Although her specialty was apple pie, Orion was partial to blackberry. She packed them full of freshly picked blackberries, a special treat that stained his teeth dark purple.

He loved to flash a big smile at his grandmother after feasting on blackberry pie, and, acting bewildered, say, "Mammaw! Mammaw! What happened to my teeth? They're rotten! Girls won't kiss me now! Oh, woe is me! (SNIFF, SNIFF, SNIFF!) I'll go through life without a kiss!"

Mammaw's laughter would shake the rafters, as she would say,

"Hush, you sweet thing. Girls will fall all over themselves just to get to you, even if you didn't have any teeth. Here, give me a big smackeroo!"

Then both would have a good laugh, the warmth of which lasted all day.

A berry hunt with Elvin was as much an exploration of hidden valleys and secret paths as it was finding the blackberries. Orion looked forward to seeing parts of Saddler Mountain that he had never seen before, and he always returned to the farm full of questions to ask Poppy John.

Elvin stuck pretty much to business on a blackberry expedition — no playing around. Actually, the old goat seldom goofed around, and he never got excited about anything. Orion had challenged him to a race earlier, but Elvin would have no part of it.

"Think about the odds, Elvin! You have four feet! I only have two!" But Elvin shook his head and turned away. By refusing to participate, Elvin let it be known that such foolish behavior was beneath his imperial status.

If Charlene was the smartest animal in the barnyard, then Elvin was the most regal. He certainly had the look of a king — dignified and sure of himself. A white goatee added to his royal appearance.

Among other things, Elvin was a finicky eater; he scrutinized every edible plant with his one good eye. Elvin had lost the other eye in a fight with a bobcat. However, the bobcat got the bad end of the deal — he ended up with Elvin's two sharp horns through his chest.

Elvin didn't mind Orion tagging along on blackberry missions. He would constantly glance around to make sure Orion was still there. When Orion fell behind, Elvin would wait until he caught up.

Elvin's closeness to Orion started late one afternoon in Shannon's Creek. Elvin had gotten his foot caught on a submerged tree limb, and his head was barely above water. Orion happened to be nearby and hear his loud cry for help.

Orion didn't waste any time. He waded in without thought for his own safety and, with water to his waist, pulled Elvin's foot free. From then on, Elvin was always nearby whenever Orion came out of the house.

Orion never knew which direction Elvin would head before starting out on a berry hunt. He only had to say, "Let's go find some blackberries, Elvin!" and away they would go.

It didn't escape Orion's attention that finding delicious blackberries depended on the whims of a goat. Although Orion would have been lost without Elvin's nose for berries, he was a little envious that a goat with only one eye knew more about Saddler Mountain than he did. However, his love of blackberries easily outweighed feelings of inferiority from playing second banana to a one-eyed goat.

As it just so happened, the path that Elvin took this morning was familiar because Orion and his grandparents walked it every Sunday to church.

A large clearing in Saddler Valley near Wilson's Branch served as an outdoor church for the Saddlers and their neighbors. On Sunday mornings, about thirty people appeared out of nowhere to listen to the Good News, sing hymns that Orion had never heard before, and share news about relatives in the surrounding mountains. He wondered where all the people came from because there wasn't a house within three miles of Poppy John's farm. He saw the churchgoers only on Sunday.

Church lasted for several hours, and then every one would disappear back into the woods on paths leading in every direction.

The church consisted of twelve pews made out of logs split in half and a ten-foot cross at the front, made of two yellow poplar saplings. Enormous live oak trees provided a natural roof as wild flowers, encircling the area, gave it color and a sense of warmth.

Worshipers didn't seem to mind the lack of a church building. During cold weather or rain, churchgoers went to the Saddler farm. A picnic — in good weather — rounded out the day's activities.

Orion didn't hide the fact that he liked the picnics much better than the preaching. The picnics gave him an opportunity to hang out with other boys and girls from the area. He developed several friendships during these outdoor gatherings.

The boys and girls wandered off after eating and either played games or talked about their week's activities.

During one Sunday afternoon, Orion held his companions spellbound by telling them about his exploration of the Pawpaw. Orion, of course, exaggerated the whole episode: "Can you imagine — taking on the Pawpaw by myself and coming out alive?"

When a young boy asked him if he was scared, Orion adjusted his belt, and said, "Of course not! There was nothing to be scared of — the sounds were only wild animals, birds, and the wind."

It was then that the older boys and girls laughed, intent on subjecting Orion to some good-natured humor. One of them said, "That's the biggest, tallest tale I've ever heard! You sure know how to tell a good one, Orion!"

Everyone agreed and had a good laugh — but the younger children wanted to hear the tale again and again.

Most of the other children had stories of unexplained noises around their farms, but none was as fascinating as Orion's conquest of the Pawpaw.

Poppy John preached several times that summer. With no regular preacher, most of the men and women took his or her time in the pulpit. Orion was fascinated the first time his grandfather preached. He sat on the back row with his mouth wide open. Orion didn't know much about the Bible, so he wondered if a lot of it was made up on the spot — a thought he never shared with his grandfather.

At various points throughout the sermon, the churchgoers would respond with shouts of "Amen, Brother Saddler!"

Poppy John was moved quite a bit too, talking loudly and swinging his arms in all directions. Orion liked when Poppy John pointed toward the congregation and declared, "There are no rest stops on the road to heaven! Amen? And there're no entertainment stops either! Amen? There're only temptation and hard times. Do I hear an amen?" Orion wanted to shout amen at the top of his lungs, but listened for the response of the crowd instead.

On the first Sunday walk to church, Poppy John stopped, pointed to the mountains in all their beauty, and said, "Take a good look around, Boy; it's not going to stay like this forever."

Orion didn't really understand the significance of the comment, although he wondered if it might have anything to do with the modern coalmine industry he had learned a little about in school. Giant machinery destroyed entire mountains to get at what some called "black gold." Coal turned out to be more valuable than real gold for many of the outsiders, but certain other mountain residents didn't realize it. They often sold their mineral rights for meager amounts, but remained poor, humble, and trusting as they watched their beloved mountains destroyed.

Orion thought to himself that he would hate to see the day come when the commercial coalmine industry would move in and destroy Saddler Mountain. Perhaps Poppy John worried about that, too.

Orion snapped back to reality long enough to make sure that Elvin was nearby, then his attention wandered back to the mountains and their beauty. Every tree, flower, shrub, and fern had colors so striking that he whimsically thought that perhaps someone ran around with a brush painting Saddler Mountain.

It hit him at that precise moment that there was not an ugly tree on Saddler Mountain. No matter how odd its shape or the color of its leaves, each tree had a symmetry and beauty of its own.

Orion shared the names of every tree and flower that Poppy John had taught him with Elvin to make the time go faster. As they came close to a group of trees, he proclaimed, "Elvin, we are now approaching perhaps the greatest stand of trees this side of the Mississippi River! Pay attention because you will be tested later."

"We have majestic scarlet oaks to the right, then the southern pines, followed by slick sumacs, black birches, sugar maples, shagbark hickories, and the most beautiful yellow poplars in the world on the left." When Orion got too loud, Elvin looked around and shook his head in disapproval.

There were always trees to share with Elvin: red, black, and sugar maples; pignuts and mockernuts; cucumber and umbrella magnolias; red, black, and scarlet oaks; beech; ashes; butternuts; black gums; sourwoods; white chestnuts; black locusts; sassafras; basswoods; ironwoods; redbuds; and pawpaws. The variety of trees in the forest impressed even a twelve-year-old boy. The trees might be small or humongous or any size in between.

Orion spotted a pawpaw tree and gasped dramatically, "Elvin! Elvin! We've found the hidden treasure of Saddler Mountain — the magnificent pawpaw! Men have spent their entire lives searching for this dazzling fruit tree. We have, my good man, found it in less than an hour. We shall go down in history as America's greatest explorers, more famous than Lewis and Clark! They'll name the tree after us. Think about it: THE ORION-ELVIN PAWPAW TREE...No wait — THE ORVIN PAWPAW TREE!"

Chirping birds were everywhere, seemingly oblivious to this one-eyed goat leading a young boy slowly up the mountain. Orion would point to the birds and bellow, "Hey, feathered creatures with wings, are you glad to see us? We're on a dangerous quest for the rare blackberry, the tastiest food on planet earth. We've gone days without food or water. But nothing will stop us! We will prevail! We will gain victory! We will find the lost blackberry patch! We will have blackberry pie! We will eat to our heart's content!"

The birds, of course, ignored him because they were on their own quest — searching for the tasty night crawler. The birds had been hunting food for several hours, and Orion wondered if the early bird really always got the worm. But he thought that being in the right spot at the right time was more important than getting there early. If you were at the wrong spot to pluck the worm, it didn't matter how early you got there.

Elvin made steady progress, stopping only once to nibble on some large green plants. Orion sat down until he finished. There was no way to speed Elvin up; he moved at his own pace.

As he waited for Elvin, Orion saw something move on the mountainside across the valley, out of the corner of his eye. He jumped up to get a better view, but it was too late. The thing, whatever it was, had been large enough to cause bushes to shake briskly as it went by. But in the blink of the eye, it was gone. He immediately roared, "That was the She-Devil! THAT...THAT...demon!"

Orion became nervous because of all the terrible stories he had heard about the She-Devil Black Panther. He didn't want to become the latest addition to her dark den.

"Elvin, did you see that?" Orion asked, as he turned for support from his berry-picking companion.

Elvin glanced at him, then continued up the path.

"I guess that's a 'no,' huh, Elvin?" Orion jokingly asked, but he was reassured by Elvin's indifference. He reasoned that if Elvin was not nervous, then he had nothing to worry about. Orion fell in behind Elvin as he went by, matching step for step.

Still, Orion kept glancing at the far hillside as they walked on. There didn't seem to be any more movement, so after a few minutes his attention turned back to discussing plants, trees, and flowers with Elvin.

A huge sassafras tree marked the spot where Elvin turned off the main trail onto a hidden path. Orion would have to remember the tree in case he ever wanted to go blackberry hunting alone. Another several hundred yards up the hill, Orion found himself in the middle of the biggest blackberry patch he had ever seen. They both dug into the berries.

"Elvin, you sly old fox, you've outdone yourself this time. It's a feast fit for a king. But then again, you are the King of Saddler Mountain, Your Highness."

Orion had learned the fine art of eating blackberries. He discovered that if he wanted to eat a lot of blackberries, he had to take it slowly. It was very important to focus on gently pulling the ripest blackberries from the vine, while clearing all other thoughts from your head. With other things on your mind, the distinctly wonderful blackberry flavor could not be enjoyed.

So for an hour and a half, Orion and Elvin ate as much of the berries as they could hold, then Orion filled a small pail to take home to Mammaw. He had no problem convincing Elvin to rest for a few minutes while he took a short nap, and then they headed for home.

When they got back to the farm, Orion couldn't wait to tell his grandfather about seeing the black panther. He ran straight to the barn, and before he could catch his breath, shouted as if he had just discovered gold, "Poppy John, I saw that old She-Devil Black Panther!"

Poppy John didn't get too excited at the news; instead, he asked Orion to describe exactly what he had seen. Orion explained precisely what had happened, adding nothing.

"Are you sure, Boy? Are you sure the wind didn't just shake the branches? No one has ever seen that Devil in daylight."

"No, sir, I'm not absolutely sure — but I saw something big and black out of the corner of my eye, going so fast that a small tree bent over as it went by. Do you think it was that old She-Devil Black Panther?"

His grandfather responded cautiously, "You can never tell what's roaming these mountains, Boy. Remember it wasn't too long ago when there was nothing but wild animals here, so anything is possible."

"I guess you're right," Orion said, realizing that Poppy John hadn't given him much of an answer.

Poppy John brought the conversation to a close by stating, "You'd just better be careful, especially when you're near Wilson's Branch."

"Yes, sir."

Orion walked away from his grandfather puzzled. He still thought he had seen the black panther and didn't understand why Poppy John did not seem to take him seriously.

He headed for his favorite thinking place beside Shannon Creek under a giant poplar tree. The running water calmed him, and the tree provided cool shade. After an hour of thought and a short nap, Orion concluded that he had in fact seen a big black animal. Satisfied that he and the black beast would cross paths again, Orion threw rocks into the moving water until it was time for supper.

Whether it was indeed the panther that he had seen that day or not, Orion had no idea then that he would have yet another bewildering encounter with a mysterious black creature of the mountains — under strange circumstances.

8

Seeing Is Believing

Totter-rot-a-nine-tenths
One-Eyed Riley
Went to the Gap on Friday
Riding old Prince,
Came back on Saturday,
Without any sense,
Totter-rot-a-nine-tenths,
Poor One-Eyed Riley.

Several weeks after the blackberry hunt with Elvin, Poppy John approached Orion with a request, "Can you go to the Gap tomorrow?"

"Me?"

"Yes. Mammaw needs more flour and corn meal."

"By myself?"

"Yes. I have to go in the other direction on church business. If you think you're ready, you can take Prince. I don't know whether he'll help or make it tougher for you."

"I'll take Prince!" Orion responded quickly. He wanted to get Prince all by himself to practice some cowboy rodeo tricks.

"Now remember, Boy, Prince knows the way to the Gap, but he has a mind of his own. From the moment you put the saddle on, you have to show him that you're the boss. When you tell him to do something, say it firmly. He has an uncanny knack for picking up a person's uneasiness. If he senses you're a pushover, he'll do what he wants rather than what you want him to do."

"Yes, sir, I'll be firm," he said. He was thinking, "Oh, Boy! I can hardly wait — 'Cowboy Orion, Bronco Champion of the Old West' rides again!"

The first time Orion had gone to the Gap with his grandfather, he didn't know what to expect. The Gap turned out to be a wide spot in the road with one building, a general store. It was there that Poppy John picked up the mail and sometimes bought dry goods for the farm. He often spent an hour or two trading stories and catching up on local news with neighbors.

Since his grandparents didn't have a car, they had to walk to the Gap. Orion had asked, "Why didn't we bring Prince? I could've ridden him."

Poppy John smiled and said, "You have to catch Prince in a good mood to ride him, but you'd be more apt to find a rainbow's end in the middle of a desert than catch him in a good mood."

He continued, "Maybe when he gets to know you better, he'll be a better saddle horse."

The far-fetched odds of riding Prince to the Gap had not dampened Orion's confidence that all he had to do was hop on him cowboy style and ride off into the sunset.

Poppy John made the trip to the Gap every week, and Orion would tag along because it gave them an opportunity to talk about any subject that came to mind. Poppy John loved to talk, and Orion loved to listen to the tales that, over time, gave Orion a strong sense of belonging in the mountains. He began to feel more and more at home.

It was on these trips that Orion learned about trees and flowers native to the region. The many mountain tales held his attention for hours. The fact that his grandfather would get him a bag of hard candy and a big dill pickle from an enormous cracker barrel made going to the Gap all the more worthwhile.

Orion went to the barn immediately after completing his chores the next morning. Mammaw had fixed several sausage and ham biscuits, smothered in blackberry jelly, to eat on the way. He tucked them safely away in the authentic western saddle bags that Poppy John had given him the night before.

As fate would have it, Orion had difficulty putting the saddle on Prince. Irritated, Prince turned around several times and stared at

Orion as if to say, "Come on, human! Do I have to put on my own saddle?" Chances are he had already sized up his young handler.

At last, Orion got the saddle on and mounted the horse. He hoped that the saddle problem would not set the tone for the whole trip. Orion thought that perhaps he should have listened more closely to Poppy John's advice about Prince rather than daydreaming of becoming a cowboy legend.

As soon as Prince got beyond the view of the farmhouse, it was clear that he wasn't the least bit interested in becoming a Wild West bronco. When Orion wanted to ride like a cowboy, Prince would slow down. The normal direction commands — Gee (to the right), Haw (to the left), and Whoa (stop) — had no effect on the horse whatsoever. Prince moved when he wanted, stopped when he wanted, and went where he wanted — all at whatever speed he wanted.

Although Prince didn't stray too far from the path, Orion soon realized the trip would take all day. Out of frustration, he ate the sausage and ham biscuits less than an hour after leaving the farm.

It wasn't long before Orion got so angry that he shouted in Prince's ear, "OK, dumbbell, do what you want. I'm out of here!" He jumped off, started to walk briskly, and was out of sight in no time flat. Ten minutes later Orion sat down to wait for the horse to catch up. Concerned when Prince didn't show up in thirty minutes, Orion went back to find him.

"Sometimes I wish I wasn't so responsible," he said kicking the ground. "But someone has to be reasonable here."

The reasonable one wasn't Prince. He had not taken a step from where Orion had left him. Orion approached him, and said, "So you didn't like to be called 'dumbbell.' How about 'Pretty Prince'?" Prince didn't acknowledge the insult; he kept on eating.

It didn't take long for Orion's attempt at humor to turn to sarcasm. "Is that more to your liking, Sir? Okay, how about Sir Pretty Prince?"

Prince continued to ignore his young companion. Orion suddenly jumped on Prince's back, as he sang a few words that he remembered of an old western song, "Back in the Saddle Again."

Prince glanced back at Orion disapprovingly. He refused to move an inch.

"Oh, so now you're a music critic!"

Orion fell silent. He didn't feel like much of a Wild West hero at the moment. Orion realized he was in the middle of a test of wills and that he was in a hopeless position. He threw up his hands and conceded: "OK, you win, big guy. We'll go to the Gap your way."

Prince started to move with a little spring in his gait as if he had been waiting to hear "you win" before taking another step. Orion thought it was a victory dance so he loudly said, "Don't rub it in, Dingledorf! Just take me to the Gap!"

Prince took him to the Gap, but it took twice as long to get there. He stopped at every grazing spot between the farmhouse and the Gap. Orion thought the horse would explode from eating so much, but fortunately he didn't.

On arriving, Orion looked around to see if anyone was looking. No one was outside the store so he mumbled, "Thank goodness for small favors," as he dismounted. He didn't want people to think he couldn't handle a horse.

Orion did not look forward to the trip back to the farm. The only good thing about the first leg of the trip was that Prince didn't bite, buck, or trample him beneath his hoofs.

Concerned because it was getting late, Orion decided to change tactics with Prince. The situation was critical. If Prince didn't speed up, they would never make it to the farmhouse before dark. And being in the mountains after dark was not smart, especially with the She-Devil Black Panther on the prowl.

Instead of fussing at Prince, Orion decided to entice him with sweetness — candy, that is. He bought several bags of candy and crossed his fingers that the candy would coax Prince to move faster on the return trip.

After shopping for Mammaw's supplies and tying the two bags to the saddle, he looked Prince in the eyes and said, "I know you understand what I'm saying, so listen: No more games! We'll be in trouble if we don't get home before dark. If I'm in trouble, you're in trouble. You have to walk faster!"

Prince neighed and shook his head.

"That's more like it!" Orion handed Prince a piece of candy, mounted him, and settled into what would become an unforgettable trip home.

The candy worked wonders as long as it lasted. When Orion ran out of candy, Prince returned to his stubborn ways. There wasn't much Orion could do about it. He tried shouting and kicking him in the side with the heel of his brogans, but nothing worked.

Orion finally decided that Prince, being a horse, couldn't foresee danger in front of his nose, and that fact put him right up there with chickens in brainpower. He noted, rather snobbishly, "You could combine your IQ with Rojo's and still come up with less than ten."

It was getting dark, and Orion held the reins tighter. He tried to adjust his eyes to the fading sunlight. He hoped Poppy John was right when he said Prince could find his way home blindfolded. To get home safely, Orion would need to trust that special ability.

In another ten minutes it was completely dark. Orion barely saw the outline of the church pews off to the right, so he knew they were at Wilson's Branch. They still had a long way to go.

Since it was dark, Prince quickened his pace, no longer stopping at every green spot on the side of the road. "Now you decide to act like a real horse," Orion said nervously.

Before Orion could say another word, a heavy blow to his head knocked him off the horse. That was all he remembered.

He didn't know how long he was out, but when he woke up he was flat on his back with a throbbing headache. He couldn't hear or see Prince anywhere.

He frantically shouted, "Prince! Prince, where are you?"

There was no response to his plea. "Just like a horse. Never around when you need them," he said, as his head ached with pain.

"All I need is a few moments," he moaned, "Then I'll be all

right."

Orion suddenly felt uncomfortable as if a thousand eyes were watching his every move.

What was he to do? He slowly extended his right hand along the ground to find what or who was there. His hand hit a furry object that made only a soft sound when he touched it, which indicated that it wasn't a threat — that was definitely a plus. Since whatever it was didn't appear to be angry, and it hadn't eaten him yet, Orion decided to open his eyes to see what it was. But he thought it best not to make any sudden moves.

The furry object was on his right, so he slowly turned his head, opening his eyes as he did. "Oh, my gosh!" he exclaimed, as he saw a huge black bear staring down at him.

The bear lifted his paw in a non-threatening way. That was good, and the bear was not showing teeth — that was even better. Then he heard some leaves rustling on his left side.

"Oh, no! There's more!" Orion said, certain his luck had run out.

As he looked in the direction of the sounds, he saw Poppy John's hound dogs — Red, Blue, and Rosie — lined up, looking at him and wagging their tails.

Orion was overjoyed, and said, "Thank goodness, I'm safe!" He then went blank again. When he woke up the three dogs were licking his face. Nothing had ever felt better. He realized that his head was lying on something soft as a cushion. For a moment he thought he was in his featherbed at the farmhouse.

The notion that he was safe in his bed quickly vanished by the sound of a snarl. It was not loud, and it didn't come from the dogs. But evidently the dogs knew what it meant because they immediately stopped licking, and they lined up again — still wagging their tails.

It didn't take an Einstein to figure out that the bear was still there. A big, slobbery lick on Orion's face confirmed it. He dared not tell the bear to stop.

He did sit up, however. The dogs' tails were wagging as fast as his heartbeat. The bear made some low noises and then stood up on her haunches. The bear was a female, about seven feet tall. She looked old and was as black as the night.

He smiled at her, and said, "Thank you, girl," thinking that it would be rude not to show some appreciation. He then started petting the dogs, repeating, "Good dogs! Good dogs!"

They were all over him, licking him like he was a long lost friend. Come to think of it, Orion was lost, and the dogs were his friends. The bear came over and offered herself for petting, too.

Orion patted her for several minutes, and then said to the dogs, "Ready to take me home?"

Red, Blue, and Rosie howled and jumped up and down.

Orion looked at the bear and said, "I'm sorry, Girl, but you can't go. I don't think Poppy John would like a bear hanging around the farm." As he gave her a big hug, something told him he had found a new friend.

As he was leaving, he saw a tree limb, partially broken, hanging over the path, and decided that was what had knocked him off Prince. He would have to come back in the daytime to cut it down.

The dogs followed the path to the farmhouse, staying close to Orion to be sure he didn't take a wrong turn. He suspected that the bear was close by all the way home.

Orion thought about the gentle bear, wondering over and over, "How could a bear and three hunting dogs get along so well together?" It was obvious they were very familiar with each other.

"Maybe they've teamed up to protect themselves against bigger and meaner beasts of the mountains," he mused.

"No, there's nothing meaner than a black bear."

Then a wild and crazy thought came to him: "What if the bear IS the She-Devil Black Panther? Or at least mistaken for one? People have seen something big and black. Why couldn't the something big and black be a bear?"

Orion remembered from the many tales about the black panther that no one had really seen her up close. "Several weeks ago, when

I saw some movement in the distance, I automatically assumed it was the black panther. But I didn't actually see a black panther."

It was all coming together now for Orion as he felt a rush of emotions come over him. "I can't prove it," he thought, "but I really think people have mistaken the bear for the black panther. Unbelievable!"

The more Orion thought about it, the more he knew he was right. He decided, though, that he shouldn't tell anyone. If he did he would have to tell them all the details — his lack of control of Prince; being whacked in the head by the tree limb; being rescued by the hound dogs; making friends with a wild bear; and on and on. People would not believe him; they'd think either he was making it all up or that the tree limb had knocked him senseless. Either way he wasn't ready for all the questioning and doubting, so the panther's true identity would become his secret. And the legend of the She-Devil Black Panther would have to remain just that — a legend.

When Orion got to the farmhouse, Mammaw was so happy to see him that he didn't have to explain anything. He told her that Prince had run off, which was more or less true, and the dogs brought him home.

He went to the barn to check on Prince. Sure enough, he was there, acting as if nothing had happened. Orion put him in the stall, taunting him, "You missed all the really good stuff! HA! HA!"

He threw his nose up at Prince, turned, and headed straight for the comfort of the featherbed. This was one night he would have no trouble sleeping.

Poppy John didn't ask for details of his trip to the Gap that night, and Orion was glad, although he knew he'd want to share them with him some day soon.

Orion drifted off to sleep, exhausted, with a smile on his face, confident he had solved the mystery of the She-Devil Black Panther — at least, as far as he was concerned — but knowing he might as well not try to convince anyone else.

9

Going Home

Orion had mixed feelings about going home. He really missed his parents, but the farm held many unforgettable memories. His relationship with Poppy John and Mammaw had deepened over the course of the summer. Since mid-July Orion ended the day with, "I love you, Mammaw. I love you, Poppy John," which was a far cry from that first night when Orion pretended to be asleep when his grandparents said "good night." No doubt, they would remain close for the rest of their lives.

It was difficult to leave the farm animals because each had become special to Orion — even Prince, the stubborn plow horse. An early goodbye to Charlene, Prince, and Elvin had left Orion unsettled. If someone had told him at the start of summer that leaving this odd collection of farm animals would be difficult, he would have laughed: "Ha! Miss a bunch of dumb animals! I don't think so!" Yet there he was, almost in tears.

Elvin had nuzzled him and walked away. Prince was his usual self — snobby and self-consumed. However, Prince let Orion hug him around the neck, which was unusual. Won over by that generous act, Orion gave him a large sweet apple.

Charlene sat on her hind legs and whined sadly as Orion walked away. But that was not surprising — she was his pet and would miss the special attention Orion heaped on her.

Looking back, Orion had much to remember — the Pawpaw, Rojo, the Black Panther legend, the enormous gentle black bear, Charlene's zest for life, berry-picking with Elvin, Sundays at the church in the woods, trips to the Gap, evenings spent on the front porch, and endless talks with Mammaw and Poppy John. Each experience, in its own way, had tested his physical and emotional limits and made him a better person.

"There's one thing I'd definitely like to forget, though!" he

91

thought, as he recalled his frightening experience in the coalmine.

The hound dogs — Red, Blue, and Rosie — had finally warmed up to Orion now that he was leaving. It was just as well because they were always in the mountains chasing something or sleeping on the porch.

The summer had heightened his appreciation of the three hound dogs, but he found that he couldn't care less if they were red-bone, ordinary, or something in-between. As Orion had told his grandfather, "A hound dog is a hound dog. A fancy name doesn't make them better than any other hound dog."

His grandfather had laughed and replied, "Now, Boy, the finer points of canine breeding take a little time to appreciate."

Since the hound dogs were always together, Orion would sometimes playfully call them "The Three Stooges," although they were far from being stupid.

One day Poppy John informed him with a smile, "There are no dogs named 'The Three Stooges' on this farm. It's an insult to those hounds!"

From then on, Orion called them by their names. It was obvious that Poppy John had a soft spot for his red-bone hound dogs.

It had surprised Orion when his grandfather told him that the dogs didn't actually belong to him, or to anyone else, for that matter: "They just showed up one day and made themselves at home." Poppy John took them rabbit and pheasant hunting in the fall, but other than that, the dogs came and went as they pleased.

The morning Orion was to leave, Mammaw fixed his favorite foods for breakfast, including apple fritters and fried apples. He tried to eat a lot of everything because it would be a long time before seeing the likes of such a breakfast again. She had spoiled him with her wonderful cooking, and it would be hard to adjust to corn flakes and an occasional egg at home.

Orion was a different boy leaving than the one who stumbled onto the farm three months ago. His visit had sharpened his physical and mental abilities. He could now work hard all day without being sore for a week. He could hoe weeds for hours on end in Mammaw's garden without breaking a sweat.

He also had less of an edge about him — that is, he didn't respond to every comment with a smart remark. He'd done a lot of thinking out on the farm, and he'd come to appreciate his parents and grandparents a lot more, and to respect those over him. He had even started to think about what he wanted to be when he grew up — perhaps a farmer like Poppy John, although college was not out of the question.

Physically, he had grown about three inches in height, had gained twenty pounds of mostly muscle, and had a deep tan from working in the sun. A bully would certainly think twice before kicking sand in his face.

The hard work had made him more confident in his abilities. There was no task on the farm — with maybe the exception of handling Old Prince — that he couldn't do, and do well. It was the kind of confidence that came from knowledge and experience, not the show-off kind that came out of a big mouth, with nothing to back it up.

There were other perhaps more important changes. For example, he had decided to give faith a chance, primarily because of attending the church in the woods and because of Poppy John's beliefs — even if he didn't totally understand them. Orion's attitude was, "If it's good enough for Poppy John, it's good enough for me."

Orion was beginning to understand that being a Saddler held special expectations on how to live his life. No one had told him, "Orion, you have to do this and that to be one of us." He just learned about the Saddler way of life by simply being close to his grandparents and watching them live their lives each day with dignity.

As a result of his grandparents' honest dealings with everyone, the Golden Rule was firmly etched into his brain. He wanted to live up to their example. Mammaw taught him to always ask himself, "Would I want to be treated that way?" before every action.

However, Orion still fell short in the category of honesty. Not having been honest with these two people who meant the world to him weighed heavily on his mind as he prepared to leave. He wished he had opened up and told Poppy John about his forbidden trek into the Pawpaw as soon as he returned home that day. But he had let it slide.

Now he regretted not being up-front with his grandfather. He had learned that it was not enough to be truthful only when asked or when caught doing something you weren't supposed to do. He felt overwhelmed by guilt.

His disobedience that day in the Pawpaw had almost cost him his life. Had it not been for Poppy John, he would have been floating face down somewhere in Shannon Creek.

Orion should have told his grandfather everything, rather than dread the moment Poppy John would discipline him for his foolish behavior.

Poppy John hadn't punished him yet, so Orion kept quiet, secretly hoping that perhaps it had been someone else with him in the Pawpaw that day. But he knew that it was only wishful thinking.

Orion remembered well the conversation on the day after his excursion into the Pawpaw, and he'd thought about it a lot:

Poppy John inquired, "Have you ever seen geese flying south for the winter in a 'V' formation?"

"I've seen pictures of them in a school book, but I've never seen the real thing."

"Do you know why they fly in that particular way?"

"No. I guess maybe it would make it more difficult to shoot them out of the sky," Orion responded.

"Well, you'd be wrong," Poppy John said, in an attempt to get Orion's attention.

Orion wondered what his grandfather was up to, but figured that he was probably leading up to the inevitable punishment. "I'd better play along," he thought.

Poppy John started his explanation more forcefully, "The geese fly in the 'V' formation because it's easier. It all has to do with the wind current created by flapping their wings, which helps the birds fly faster and longer. Only the lead goose has a hard job, but when he gets tired another bird takes over. That way every bird takes his turn at doing the hard work."

Orion didn't know why Poppy John was telling him about a bunch of geese. He didn't know what to say, so he listened.

"That's not all. The geese all honk loudly in order to encourage the birds in front to keep up their speed. And if a bird gets hurt or sick and falls out of formation, two other birds stay with him until he gets better."

"What do you think about the geese, Orion?"

"I'm not exactly sure."

Orion realized that Poppy John was making a point, but he was not sure what it was. He thought, "How can geese do anything that humans should think about?" But he dared not mention that to Poppy John because it was obvious he wanted to teach him something.

Poppy John stared at Orion, but didn't say anything. The silence made Orion uneasy, so he thought he'd better say something, even if it was wrong: "Well, the geese seem smart enough — for birds. But why would two birds follow a sick one while the rest of the formation keeps on going? By doing that, three geese are lost from the flock instead of one. Is that smart?"

Poppy John looked sternly at Orion as he shook

his head and said, "You think about the geese some more. I'm sure you'll come up with something else."

He started to walk away, turned back around and smiled at Orion, then went on the barn.

***

Since Mammaw would not be accompanying them down the mountain to meet his father at the highway, her goodbye was especially hard for Orion. Both sobbed unashamedly and hugged each other tightly before, at Poppy John's urging, they were able to pull away from each other.

Although Orion would definitely miss Mammaw's cooking, there was so much more about her to remember. Her gentle, caring nature and fun-loving wit had led him to enjoy the company of a female, something he never thought possible.

As he threw his clothes bag over his shoulder, he took one last look at the barn and saw Mammaw standing on the porch. He heard her trembling voice say, "Orion, make sure you eat a good breakfast!"

He didn't turn around because he knew he would cry, so he shouted over his shoulder, "I will, Mammaw," as he rounded the far end of the house.

At the last point on the trail where the farmhouse was visible, Orion turned, gave a sigh, and turned his thoughts to home back in Ohio. He sensed that he had changed, but didn't know exactly how or how much.

The trip over the mountain was uneventful, but full of images for Orion, as he tried to remember everything of the past summer. As they walked, Poppy John tested him on his knowledge of trees, flowers, and plants. Orion passed with flying colors.

"I see you've been studying, Boy. You're better than I am!"

Orion could hardly contain his desire to burst out with a delighted laugh on hearing that compliment, but managed to respond with only a smile and the proper amount of humility, "I practiced a lot this summer with Elvin."

"Indeed you did!"

As they passed Shannon's Branch, Poppy John stopped momentarily, bowed his head, and simply asked God for a safe trip home for his son and grandson. Orion was deeply touched by his grandfather's thoughtfulness, saying only, "Thank you, Poppy John."

Poppy John smiled and said, "That's so you can come back next summer."

"I wouldn't miss it for the world!"

Later as they came down the east side of the mountain, Orion saw his father standing beside the car. There was something unfamiliar about his father. He had never seen him in quite the same way. Had his father changed? Had he gotten taller? Orion kept an eye on his father as he continued down the path.

Not knowing if his father could hear him, he yelled, "Here we are! Here we are!" His father looked in his direction and waved. Orion picked up his pace. When he reached his father, he stuck out his hand and said, "I've really missed you!"

"I've missed you, too!"

And then they hugged each other. Holding him at arms' length, his father proudly observed, "Look at you! I'm impressed. Let me see those muscles!"

Orion flexed his muscles as they both laughed. Poppy John caught up with them and gave his son a big hug. The first thing Poppy John told Jesse was, "You have a great son! I don't think I could have made it without Orion's help."

Orion couldn't believe his ears. Poppy John had called him by his name. To him it meant that he was officially no longer a boy. It was an honor coming from his grandfather he felt he had earned.

The three of them spent a few minutes by the side of the car talking, telling tales, and catching up. Orion looked back longingly at the mountain that he and his grandfather had just crossed. Sadness overtook him, and he started to tear up until he thought, "Things will be even better next year."

Poppy John walked over and gave Orion a big hug and said, "I love you, Orion. Take care of yourself so you can come back and help me next year."

Orion found that he wasn't embarrassed by hearing an adult say, "I love you," to him in front of somebody else. It was one indication how far he had come under the guidance of loving grandparents.

"I love you, too, Poppy John. Thanks for the greatest summer a boy could ever have!"

When Jesse got in the car, Orion asked him to wait there just a minute; he walked a few feet away and motioned for Poppy John. His heart thumping loudly, his voice quivering, he managed to say quietly, "Poppy John, I want to thank you for saving my life in the Pawpaw."

"Are you sure it was me?" Poppy John replied.

"Oh, I'm sure. I saw the red bandana hanging from your back pocket."

"Fair enough. But plenty of men wear red bandanas in their pockets around here."

"Sure! But anyway, I want you to know that I know I disobeyed you, and I am truly sorry; and I'm sorry I wasn't man enough to admit it at the time. And I want you to know that the geese story was not lost on me. It finally struck me that a person doesn't accomplish anything worthwhile alone. You need other people around to encourage you to keep going and to care for you when you get into trouble."

"I figured you had learned your lesson. That's why I didn't mention it at the time."

Orion teased his grandfather: "So you admit it! How else did you know I was in the Pawpaw if you weren't the one who saved me?"

"Maybe a little birdie told me," Poppy John answered, with a grin.

As Poppy John walked him back to the car, Orion asked him to take good care of Charlene. Poppy John laughed and said, "Oh, don't worry. I'll take good care of her. For a minute or two back at the farm, I thought you were going to bring her with us."

Jesse looked at both of them quizzically, saying only, "Huh?" Poppy John winked at Orion and offered, "Orion will tell you all about it in the car."

Jesse smiled and said, "Let's go, Orion — we have a long trip ahead of us." With that, Orion hurriedly gave Poppy John one last hug and jumped in the car. He waved to Poppy John as they pulled on to the highway.

He watched the giant figure by the side of the road until he was out of sight, then turned and said to his father, "I think Poppy John is crying."

"I know. You made a big impression on him, Orion. That's the first time I've seen him cry since my brother, Miles, got killed in the war. You remind Poppy John of him."

Orion sighed, laid his head on the back of the seat, and within minutes fell asleep.

When he awoke, Orion was glad that the trip was nearly half over. His father asked him about Charlene. Orion went through the whole story from the moment he saw her to the ten-dollar purchase price and work agreement. He expected a reprimand from his father for spending his money foolishly, but Jesse listened carefully. Orion was surprised at his father's words when he finished: "It's your money, and it's your decision how to spend it. Make sure you send Poppy John the ten dollars as soon as we get home." With those words, the issue was settled and was never mentioned again.

For a long while, Orion continued to talk about his summer adventures. Somehow it seemed hard to imagine that his father was immediately able to relate to most of his experiences, since he'd grown up on Saddler Mountain himself. Yet as he stopped to think about it, Orion suddenly felt a connection to his father that he'd never had before.

As Jesse's attention turned back to driving, Orion's thoughts drifted to school. He only had three days until school started. One thing he knew for sure was that it was going to be different this year. Orion had decided not to sleep in class anymore; he discovered that he really wanted to learn all he could about the world. And also Orion had decided not to run with any kids who didn't take school seriously; he didn't want be one of a bunch of losers.

Orion smiled as he thought that the old gang would not know him when he returned to school. They might even try to tease or torment him about the changes, but it wouldn't bother him now. He knew that he was strong enough to take a stand for what he believed in if necessary.

Orion knew that homework would now have to be done and studying for tests would become a priority. There would be no question he'd help out at home. He wanted to become all he could be. He wanted to make his parents and grandparents proud, and he wanted to continue to have a sense of pride in himself, like that he'd discovered by doing his chores well on the farm.

Orion knew he was different now. He'd become a better person that summer on Saddler Mountain — and he kind of liked that person he'd become.

THE END

Woodland Press, LLC

Appalachian Authors. Appalachian Stories.
Appalachian Pride.

www.woodlandpress.com

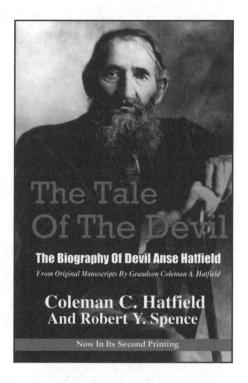

Order This Popular Woodland Press Title Today:

The Tale of the Devil:
The Biography of
Devil Anse Hatfield

By Dr. Coleman C. Hatfield and Robert Y. Spence

HARDBACK

Order at http://www.woodlandpress.com
or call: (304) 752-7500

Reseller/Wholesale Programs Available

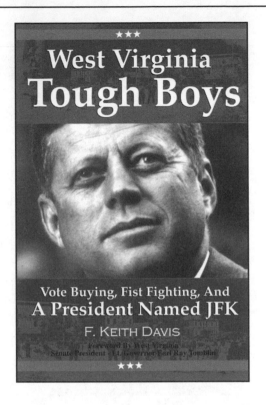